AMERICA 2014
AN ORWELLIAN TALE

BY DAWN BLAIR

Progressive Source Publishing

FIRST EDITION

Printed in Canada.

Design and Illustration by Sammy Yuen, Jr.

ISBN 157-178-175-7

Library of Congress Control Number: 2004095457

For bulk rates or additional information, go to America2014.com

ONE

Winston Smith ambled out of the Chambers Street subway station like a young man who could afford to take his time. He stepped aside to let the city workers rush past on their way to work, and turned to see the large video billboard mounted along the side of the subway entrance.

Winston enjoyed watching the Homeland Security public service announcements that he created, and one of his favorite shorts had just begun. On the billboard, a military marching tune played as a full-screen American flag waved in the breeze, with giant words superimposed over it that read, "In God's United States, Homeland Security is Watching Out For You." The flag morphed into the stern, aged face of Homeland Security General John Bashcrost, and the words "In God's United States. Homeland Security is Watching You." The five-foot image then became an enormous mirror, reminding viewers that cameras embedded in the billboards were monitoring every move they made.

Winston stared into the mirror. He was surprised that he looked anxious, and realized that the meeting he was heading to was making him uncharacteristically nervous. He quickly adjusted his expression for the surveillance cameras, trying to appear more upbeat. Looking in the mirror made him more comfortable. A bit over six feet tall, he looked young for twenty-nine, and the time he'd spent at the gym had paid off with a well-toned frame. His short, slightly gelled hair reflected the latest young businessman's style, hip but respectful. He was ready to roll.

As he arrived on lower Broadway, Winston could see the glistening green glass tower of the federal office building. It rose majestically over the soot-encrusted old city buildings surrounding it. As he reached the security buffer zone, which started a full block from the building, a few dozen people were already waiting. Winston had allowed plenty of time. He took off his black silk Armani suit jacket, and laid it carefully over his shoulder as he patiently lined up behind the others.

A very skinny Chinese delivery man, about eighteen years old and wearing a food-stained white shirt, tugged lightly at Winston's arm from behind. Holding out a delivery slip stapled to a bag of food, he tapped the address scrawled there, nodded his head inquisitively, and asked Winston, "Good?"

Winston read the federal building address on the paper and nodded, "This is the address. You must line up here and present your ID. You have your ID?"

The Chinese man shook his head uncomprehendingly and forced a nervous grin, revealing a mouthful of misshapen teeth. Winston rolled his eyes. The poor guy barely knew two words of English, he thought. He turned away, but the man was persistent. He tapped on the address on the bag again, and said, "Good, yes?"

"Yes, address good, yes, good," Winston said impatiently, pointing to the federal skyscraper nearby. "But you **must** have identification, understand, identification . . ."

The deliveryman nodded vigorously. "Address good, yes!"

Winston was relieved that a green light announced his turn to proceed. An arrow directed him into one of three fully automated "STOP FOR SEARCH" lanes, which were surrounded by a series of heavily armored guard stations.

As Winston approached the red line on a "STOP FOR SEARCH" lane, a Predator sniffer drone hovering overhead dropped down, then darted around him like a bee, scanning for weapons, explosives, or nuclear or chemical material. Although the titanium-armored drone was not much larger than his briefcase, it was a menacing device, with a laser blaster fixed on his body at all times.

"Your name and purpose, please," a pleasant woman's voice asked from the sniffer drone.

"Winston Smith to see the Federal Communications Commission Director of Compliance Neil Swan for a nine o'clock appointment."

"Please look up at a forty-five degree angle."

The drone performed a retina scan, accessed Neil Swan's visitor schedule, then matched Winston's scan with his file from Homeland Security's national identity database.

A green light flashed at a narrow, freestanding printout station right next to Winston. "Mr. Smith, please remove your visitor badge from the slot to your left and proceed directly to the lobby and the forty-eighth floor," the drone said.

As Winston took his badge, he heard a commotion in the security lane next to him and turned to watch what was going on. Another sniffer drone in that lane was darting around the Chinese deliveryman at an incredibly high speed. The man flailed his food bag around his head trying to keep the drone back. "Refusal to present identification for the third time," a menacing voice barked from the sniffer drone. "This is the fourth and last warning: present valid identification within twenty seconds or immediate termination will follow!"

The drone near Winston suddenly appeared in his sightline. It spoke with the same woman's voice he had heard before, but this time with a sense of urgency. "A security matter is being resolved and does not concern you. You must proceed to the lobby immediately!"

Winston clipped on his ID badge and walked straight ahead. He heard what sounded like a long, loud surge of an electrical current in the lane next to him, then the Chinese man screaming in pain. He was struck by the unmistakable stench of burning flesh, but he dared not turn to look. He suppressed an impulse to vomit, and continued walking. His sniffer drone hovered silently beside him, its laser focused on Winston's head, until he got to the cool glass skyscraper.

Winston inserted his visitor badge into a slot and a door opened into the air-conditioned lobby of the federal office building. He walked past another armored sentry post to the guest entry turnstile. A white-haired guard in a blue blazer turned from a video monitor of the outside area and looked over Winston's visitor's badge.

"What . . . what happened?" Winston asked, stunned.

The guard shook his head angrily. "Cheap fucken greasy spoon!" he cursed. "How stupid can you get, sending an idiot who can't speak English through a drone-managed security zone. That's the second time this month. I can tell you that nobody's gonna order from that fucken place again!"

DAWN BLAIR

Two

On the elevator to the forty-eighth floor, Winston wondered whether he ought to mention the sniffer drone incident to his boss Neil Swan. As one of the most powerful federal officials in the building, Swan might be able to influence the security protocol.

Then again, Winston thought, security was security, and the deliveryman had been asked, in plain English, for his identification. Swan wasn't likely to sympathize with an immigrant who had managed to get into the country despite his ignorance of the English language. Winston didn't want Swan to think he was becoming a "whiner." He didn't want *that* to turn up in his Homeland Security file.

Neil Swan hated whiners. Like Federal Communications Commission Chairman Russ Limetoff, Swan enforced a "Top Ten-only" rule about subjects that merited complaints. The rule was that liberals, pinkos, foreigners, special interests, queers, femi-nazis, enviro-nazis, racialists, baby-killers and whiners were fair game—keep your mouth shut about anything else, especially anything to do with government policy or national security.

Winston stepped off the elevator into the large, wood-paneled reception area for the F.C.C. Compliance Department, announced himself to the receptionist, and was asked to take a seat. He was twenty minutes early, and Swan was always at least twenty minutes late. The meeting needed to move quickly to an important approval stage, Winston realized, with no time for whining. He resolved to forget about the drone incident and focus on his own problems.

Winston's pulse quickened and he began feeling nauseated. He had never been nervous at meetings with Neil Swan before. But a sense of failure now swept through his belly. Was it a premonition?

Swan had advised Winston never to get emotionally invested in any single issue or project, explaining, "Our Nationalist Party commitment must be to a broader political vision—wars and issues and projects change, vision does not."

Winston couldn't have cared less about wars, or issues. But projects . . . projects were personal. He hoped that he would look back on the day's meeting as a milestone in his fast-rising career.

It was up to Swan to provide the final go-ahead for the project that Winston had been working on for more than two years. It was a remake of George Orwell's *1984*, set in the Islamic fundamentalist Republic of Iran, thirty years later, in present day 2014.

The *1984* remake would allow Winston to move from writing and producing Homeland Security commercials to his first full-length propaganda film. To him, this was more than another high-paying career advancement prior to his thirtieth birthday. *1984* would be the first project in his life that Winston could consider a real labor of love, a project that he had been called—perhaps even born—to make.

As a patriotic member of the Nationalist Party, Winston was required to attend church services almost every Sunday, but he did not consider himself a religious person. Still, he believed that it was his unique fate that brought him to update *1984*.

Winston had been born in 1984, to liberal parents who happened to be named Smith. The naming of their son for the protagonist of Orwell's novel started as a political statement against the Reagan administration. To Winston, however, his name had taken on a very different meaning on September 11, 2001, when his father was one of nearly 3,000 people murdered by terrorists in the World Trade Center attacks.

Although not yet seventeen, Winston had been old enough to conclude that the liberalism which had marked his parents' views was dead forever. His career in conservative media started immediately, as a victims' family representative speaking out about the need for preemptive war in Afghanistan and Iraq. During college a few years after his father's death, Winston became an intern at Foxy News. There he worked for Neil Swan, the powerful producer who was to become his political guardian and advisor.

It was Swan who later helped him secure his first draft deferment, based upon the work he was doing for the Nationalist Party and Homeland Security Agency. "This war is important to our country," Swan had explained, shortly after the United States began its long war of occupation in Pakistan and reinstated the draft. "But so are men like you."

Winston tried to take his mind off the meeting and relax. He looked over the impressive wood-paneled reception area, and tried to imagine how different the offices that now housed the national headquarters of the Federal Communications Commission Compliance Department's must have looked ten years earlier, when they had been the regional offices of the Environmental Protection Agency. Swan had once described the previous décor as "bureaucratic steel-cabinet shithole."

Swan enjoyed telling Winston, during some of their private meetings, about how he and F.C.C. Chairman Russ Limetoff had led the campaign to defund the "enviro-nazis" at the E.P.A. Swan himself had managed the effort to "relegate the enviro-nazis to the dustbin of history," which succeeded even before the revised Constitution outlawed the Democratic Party.

Like many of the most important steps in the Blush Administration's "Patriotic Restoration" campaign, the decision to defund the E.P.A. took place in a party committee room. A year after the 2006 midterm elections, during which the Nationalist Party won control of more than two-thirds of the seats in both the House and Senate, all federal budget decisions moved to Nationalist Party meeting rooms and the lucrative "Industry Consultation" sessions that Vice President Dick Croney had popularized. Attendance and all related records became Top Secret for national security, but the conclusions were widely publicized once they became law. By 2008, the E.P.A. had become a victim of the urgent need for more tax cuts, rising payments on the national debt, and funding for an ever-expanding War on Terror.

Corporate America had been delighted, Winston recalled, feeling a bit better, and the speaking fees of top federal officials increased exponentially. Vice President Croney, whose income that year was rumored to top one hundred million dollars, was paid five million dollars just to appear at the American Petroleum Association's annual dinner, setting a world record for a speaking fee honorarium.

Even Winston, who had just begun his career making public service ads, had received more than two hundred thousand dollars in "Party Consulting" checks that year. He wondered how much Neil Swan earned. Russ Limetoff, he knew, was in the centimillion earnings category, and he had heard that Swan was the highest-paid Director in the agency. Of course, Winston realized, salary and bonus would only be a fraction of the speaking and consultation fees that the Party would throw Swan's way . . .

"The Director is running about twenty minutes late," the receptionist said, standing over Winston's armchair and interrupting his calculations.

He thanked her and became anxious about the meeting again. He reassured himself that there was nothing to worry about. He had played his cards right from the very beginning, seeking Swan's counsel on the very notion of writing and producing the remake of *1984*. Swan could have killed the project with a word. Instead Swan was, as always, supportive of Winston's aspirations. "Communism may be dead and buried, but what Orwell described is no worse than what they have in the unliberated territories of Iran today," Swan had said, green-lighting the development effort.

No movie or TV show got made in God's United States without the approval of Neil Swan's Department of Compliance. It oversaw the content of billions of dollars worth of public service announcements, as well as all private newspapers, magazines, web sites, electronic games—even comic books. Thousands of F.C.C. Compliance employees at satellite offices in Los Angeles, Seattle, Miami and other major cities followed Swan's directives, as he insured that the nation's entertainment was sufficiently patriotic and free of subversive material. The Party had a responsibility to the people to protect them in the War on Terror and the media had a responsibility to communicate this, to allow its citizens to understand and provide their government with what F.C.C. Chairman Russ Limetoff called "Patriotically Informed Consent."

Apart from Russ Limetoff, and the President's Communications Director Anne Culture, Director of Compliance Neil Swan was the most powerful media figure in God's United States. Yet he found time to meet Winston once every two weeks, treating him almost like a surrogate son.

Winston noticed that he was sweating, and wiped his brow. He cursed himself for being so nervous, and repeated the words in his mind, like a mantra, "routine meeting, routine meeting."

It didn't help. Maybe he had made a mistake hiring Paul Goode, his old college flatmate from the semester Winston had spent in London. Paul was an Orwell scholar, and had been a useful consultant when it came to adapting some of the author's political views. But Paul was also a news producer for BBC TV, a network notorious for its anti-Americanism. Had someone in Compliance noted that?

Or perhaps the problem was his recent script change, in which he had made the woman loved by the protagonist in his version of *1984* a doctor instead of a party hack. Would Russ think this was too "feministic" a change?

Winston's thoughts were interrupted by Swan's assistant. "The Secretary will see you now, Mr. Smith," she said.

She escorted Winston down the quiet corridor to a well-appointed corner office the size of a large conference room. It provided a sweeping view of Lower Manhattan and the Hudson River, and held nearly every media presentation device in use, all seamlessly integrated into a voice-activated system. The bookshelves were crammed with media awards and Nationalist Party trophies, while the antique wood-paneled wall was covered with framed photos of Neil Swan with hundreds of different celebrities and politicians, including at least a half dozen shots with President Blush.

Swan looked thinner in the photos than in the flesh. Still, at nearly six feet tall and some three hundred fifty pounds, he commanded a powerful presence. Hair growth treatment and coloring disguised nearly all the gray and bald spots on Swan's round head, and only the rings of fatty wrinkles around his neck revealed that Swan was pushing sixty.

Swan pointed Winston toward an armchair across from his enormous, file-covered desk. His secretary brought Swan a fresh cup of coffee, and, without needing to ask, set a fine crystal tumbler of Winston's favorite beverage on a coaster in front of him.

"Please close the door, Cynthia," Swan asked politely.

Winston had not expected the meeting to require a closed door. A wave of worry crashed inside his head. He noticed that his hand was shaking and slipped it into his pocket.

Swan's eyes darted knowingly from Winston's hand to his

eyes. He greeted Winston politely, smiled for a moment, and then his face tightened for business. "Let me get right to the point, Winston. You have done important work for our country," his eyes glanced over Winston's Junior Pioneer badge, representing a two hundred thousand dollar annual pledge to the Nationalist Party, and Winston was pleased that he had worn it. "Russ and I—and the Party—know that you will continue to do great work for the country. But I can't help you this time."

Swan tossed Winston's *1984* script across the table at him. "This is competent work. But I just spoke with Susan Giccanti at the network, and let her know that we have to cancel the project."

"But . . . but I made all the recommended changes and . . ."

"It's D.B.A., son: Dead Before Arrival. Shred the scripts, and whatever copies of the books that you have. It's time to move on."

Winston was devastated. He had worried that there might be a scheduling delay. But this was far worse.

"Neil, please, I know I have no right to this, but could you please . . . you know?"

Swan flicked a manual switch beneath his desk that froze all recording devices. It was a privilege that only the very highest government and business officials enjoyed.

Swan announced his preamble from memory. "You are not entitled to this information, and any unauthorized disclosure of this decision by the Compliance Department will result in your arrest and indefinite incarceration under Section 52 of Patriot Act VI. But since this is already declassified and is being announced by Secretary Limetoff on tonight's news shows, there is nothing to stop me from informing you that the Federal Communications Commission is being renamed the Ministry of Truth. Russ likes the ring to it, especially Minister of Truth, and both the President and Mr. Croney want to market the *truth* word more vigorously. You know, the Federal Trade Commission has had the F.T.C. acronym forever, so we can't call ourselves the Federal Truth Commission. Ministry works better than Commission, anyway, don't you think?"

Swan smiled as he scanned Winston's face for any hint of dis-agreement. Winston worked hard not to express the anxiety that was throbbing in his head.

"But what about the book? It's widely available and in many schools required read—" Winston realized, a moment too late, that he was pushing it.

Swan shook his head, annoyed, and switched the recording device back on. "As you and every informed Patriotic Citizen in or out of the entertainment industry should know, this Office will make no comments on books or other printed work that may or may not be subversive. Remember that Section 52 of Patriot Act VI mandates that the act of directing follow-up questions about censored, possibly censored, or uncensored work to officials of the Federal Communications Commission Department of Compliance is a crime punishable by an indeter-minate prison sentence."

"I . . . I understand fully, Mr. Swan."

Swan relaxed his face, switched the recording devices off again, and returned to his sympathetic demeanor. "Call me Neil, son."

"I'm terribly sorry about all this, Neil, but I had hoped . . ."

"No need to apologize, Winston. Compliance is compliance, and in Time of War, it sometimes happens unexpectedly." Swan glanced at his watch. "So . . . have you considered taking some of that vacation time you've been accumulating while working like a true GOB-ber for your country and Party?"

"Uhh—I hadn't considered it. I guess a vacation could be nice."

"I recommend Las Vegas. A good patriotic town. Been there lately?"

"Not in a few years."

"What's not in Las Vegas? Paris, only cleaner, and without the back-stabbing French. Canals like Venice, with no thieves, and Italian food that's better—and cheaper. You want outdoors? There's a new simulated climb of Mount Everest, complete with sherpas and even grimy guesthouses, at the Palace Hotel. And I don't need to tell you about the Happiness Cocktails—or the girls!"

Winston forced a smile. "Thank you for the suggestion, Neil."

"I've already spoken with your supervisor and had it approved. We'll be doing a bit of housework for the agency renaming anyway, and you just delivered a great commercial, so it's a good time to take three entire restful, and maybe even sinful weeks!"

Swan winked and smiled. He stood up, escorted Winston to the door, and gave him a strong, smothering bear hug. "Don't worry, son, you'll make a film one day. Chalk this one up to experience. Meanwhile, enjoy Las Vegas—live a little!"

THREE

Winston's legs felt numb as he headed back to the Chambers Street subway station. He would have taken a cab to his office at Columbus Circle, but that would have meant at least an hour extra in midtown traffic. He pulled off his jacket and loosened his tie as he walked along the hot, litter-strewn sidewalk.

He was already wet with sweat by the time he climbed down into the dirty subway platform. The air in the station was as stifling as a sauna. It was ninety-seven degrees outside and twenty degrees warmer on the platform. The sultry heat was unusual for a morning in March, even for 2014, which had already broken the heat records set the year before. The New York subway system was no closer to air conditioning its platforms than it had been fifteen years before, when Winston was a teenager using the same station to get home from high school. President George Blush had recently advised that "Global warming has certain advantages," but one hundred twenty-degree subway platforms, Winston thought, was not one of them.

His briefcase felt heavy. He set it on the ground, and wished there was a bench to sit on, like there had been when he was young. Thoughts pounded in his head. Was the project really doomed? He telephoned Susan Giccanti, his company's head of TV films, to try to arrange an emergency meeting. Muting the video input so that nobody would see how distraught he looked, he spoke with Danielle, Susan's assistant, who told him that Susan was booked all day. Winston pleaded for a short sit-down. Danielle promised to get back to him.

A nearby video billboard mounted on a steel pillar provided a welcome distraction from his anxiety. An ad for Foxy News, Winston's former employer, appeared. It was mostly a war news-reel of "sexy kills," with footage of missiles hitting targets, heli-copter attacks, tanks advancing on enemy positions in desert coun-tries, and Predator drones firing on guerillas in the jungles of Indonesia. "Duty takes our boys to fight. Foxy lets you go with them!" the voice track proudly announced, over the din of explo-sions and war machines.

A couple of street-smart teen boys, one wearing a tee shirt from nearby Stuyvesant High School—Winston's alma mater—shuffled up next to him to watch the action on the video screen. The war video morphed into generals at a press briefing, then President Blush himself, being interviewed by Bob O'Manley, his Secretary of State, on the popular talk show that O'Manley still hosted. "The Patriotic Citizen's source for all news," the voice track continued. "Radio, Broadcast and Interactive TV. News when you want it. Balanced. Patriotic. Fair. Foxy: The Only Name in TV News™."

"Oh, right, they're the only name in news and they're bal-anced and fair," one of the boys said to his friend, sticking out a studded tongue in disgust. "Fair means we get to die and they make sure no dead or wounded bodies ever appear on TV."

"What a pit of shit," the other kid said, looking at Winston, suspicious yet defiant. "'Course they're the only name in news— they fucken shut down everyone else. They can take their draft and shove it!"

Before Winston could challenge them, the kids ran down the platform and hopped onto a local train. Winston was too upset by his own problems to try to report them and besides, if Homeland Security wanted them, then Homeland Security could track them down using surveillance footage. He was surprised that they knew about Foxy's "no dead or wounded" policy, and realized that their parents must have been violating the Home Discussion provisions of Patriot Act VI by teaching their kids about it.

Although he was more than a little impressed by their defiance, Winston doubted that the boys would be so brave when they got to be a few years older, when resisting the draft would mean ten years in a prison labor camp or a lifetime of self-imposed exile in a dangerous, unmonitored urban ghetto.

They would learn the hard way, Winston thought, as he himself had, that the idealism of the rebel dies fast in the real world. Unless their parents were big Party donors, or unless they became indispensable members of the Party, they'd be singing a different tune when the draft board police buses arrived at the end of their high school graduation ceremony.

Winston had been older than that when the draft was reinstated in 2006, and well into graduate school. At the time, he supported President Blush's decision to "stay the course," and militarily confront the potential terrorism of a newly elected Islamic fundamentalist government in Pakistan. With an occupation going badly in Iraq and Iran, the move on Pakistan required hundreds of thousands of new soldiers.

Winston agreed with the need for a draft, but he told himself that he had more important skills to contribute to his country. He had worked his way up in the Young Nationalist league while at Columbia Journalism school. That, plus his internship at Foxy News, had brought relationships that helped him avoid the annual draft lotteries that were quickly implemented to replace tens of thousands of military casualties every year.

Foxy News had perhaps saved Winston's life, and it had been a great career builder for both him and his boss Neil Swan. Like many officials doing public service in the Blush Administration, Swan was allowed to keep his industry job at Foxy, while serving in Russ Limetoff's aggressive Federal Communications Commission. In 2010, Patriot Act VI and the new Patriotic Citizen's Constitution gave the F.C.C. the authority to assess which TV and radio networks were "sufficiently patriotic to deserve the privilege of using the public airwaves or public Internet." They found only Foxy, and its recently acquired Clear Channel Communications radio empire, to be worthy of retaining their broadcast licenses. Every other source of video, radio and Internet news in God's United States was shut down. It was then that Foxy had cleverly evolved its logo to "Foxy: The Only Name in News™."

Some had openly protested. Public demonstrations, in the revised Constitution's new Bill of Rights and Responsibilities, brought ten-year mandatory sentences at privatized prison labor camps in Time of War. The officers and employees of organizations like the A.C.L.U., the Natural Resources Defense Council, the Drug Policy Alliance and Planned Parenthood, groups that Homeland Security General Bashcrost determined had sympathized with terrorists, challenged patriotism, or "impeded government functions," were treated with similar severity. Millions of members of these organizations were visited by Homeland Security troopers, F.B.I. agents, or local police. Those who were not sent to jail for failing on-the-spot drug tests for marijuana traces from their hair samples were given the choice of signing denunciations of the work of the organization they had belonged to, or facing ten year mandatory sentences. A surprising number of Americans had refused to sign the statements, and the population of the prison labor camps grew by millions.

Winston and his department worked overtime for months to explain, through public service ads, the necessity of the strict new media and speech legislation. "Empowering patriotism," Neil Swan had called the campaign trumpeting the changes. Some old-timers, like Winston's mother, objected privately, and left the country. Winston parroted the Party line during their last meeting, arguing that Americans needed to stop dwelling on their own petty differences and start thinking of how they might help secure the greater good now that the War on Terror had changed everything.

Winston's thoughts returned to the present and he found himself gazing at a video billboard waiting for one of his ads to rotate through. His work, he reminded himself, helped reach that greater good, even if the short Homeland Security commercials he created were not as prestigious as full-length movies.

One of his recent ads began with the flag waving in the breeze and small letters expanding across the screen to read, "God's United States: The Freest Country on Earth™."

The narration played over images of children checking books out of a library, then a woman reading a newspaper in a comfortable home. "In America, everyone is free to read or watch whatever he or she chooses. Patriotic Citizens, of course, restrict their media and Internet usage to materials that do not promote subversive, treasonous, or terrorist ideas and actions." The video showed a bearded, Jewish-looking man with glasses and an enormous glowing "S" hanging over his chest reading a computer monitor that read "Restricted Access" in large letters. "Our society," the narration continued, "is so tolerant that some people—those who register as Subversives—are even free to read unpatriotic and foreign materials! But be vigilant—because even freedom has its limitations. Remember, Subversives are never allowed to distribute information to Patriotic Citizens, and accepting such materials is a federal crime!" The video concluded with the bearded man on a deserted street corner handing a woman a pamphlet titled, *Why the World Hates America*. A moment after the woman accepted the pamphlet, a squad of Homeland Security troopers appeared out of nowhere and roughly arrested both of them.

Winston wondered whether the arrest scene was too tough. He thought of the stench of the dying Chinese deliveryman. A sudden fit of nausea twisted in his stomach and erupted in a fit of coughing. He just managed to make it to the edge of the platform and vomited onto the tracks.

He worried as he spit out the bitter aftertaste of his breakfast and wiped his mouth. Was he participating in what his mother, before he blocked her calls, had characterized as the government's "deliberate desensitization" to violence against its own citizens? Or was he just getting soft?

The old steel wheels of an "A" express train gave out a deafening screech as it pulled into the station. Winston boarded and sat in the center of a long bench in the near-empty subway car, within view of a large video billboard, and thought carefully about Swan's canceling of his project. Like most business decisions, he told himself, it probably had nothing to do with him and everything to do with circumstances beyond his control—the renaming of the agency.

The video billboard loudly began a public service ad that his friend Slim had been bragging about in the company dining hall earlier in the week. Slim's job, Winston recalled, as he put on his best poker face for the surveillance cameras behind the billboard, was to explain how the Party's economic policies worked for all Americans, despite record high unemployment, with three-quarters of the population uninsured, Medicare bankrupt, and half the federal budget going to pay interest on an expanding federal debt.

The narrator in the ad was a handsome New York policeman

in a crisp blue uniform. "Today, the tax bill of the average millionaire is three times that paid by the average police officer," the officer said, as he morphed into three police officers, with addition symbols between them. At the end of this equation was an equal sign, and then the image of a well-to-do executive in a suit. The officer continued. "That's okay, but, in Time of War, when our great nation needs every job it can get, why should those millionaires **also** be burdened with additional social security taxes for the servants they are patriotic enough to hire? That sounds like class warfare to me! And I thought that went out with the Democrats!" The video shifted to a professorial man standing behind a lectern, with the caption "Economist" at the bottom of the screen. "Not every vestige of class warfare went out when Subversive political parties were banned," the economist explained. "Updating our tax law takes time—and commitment." The economist continued his narration, as legions of domestic workers, of all races and ages, marched past a flowing American flag. "Thousands more tax-paying gardeners, cooks, butlers, housekeepers and nannies could be hired, if only the wealthy among us could be liberated from these excessive taxes." The policeman returned to conclude, "Congress is debating an end to domestic servant taxes. V-mail your elected Party representative, and tell him that in 2014, class warfare no longer makes dollars and sense!"

Winston wondered why the government bothered running such ads, when Congress would vote unanimously, as they always did, for the Party's tax cut. Even though opposition politics in Washington had been, in the words of General Bashcrost, "rendered quaint" by the War on Terror, Winston guessed that the Party wanted to remind its super-wealthy contributors that the Blush Administration was always looking out for their interests. Using taxpayer money for public service ads was cheaper than running Party fund-raising commercials, he thought cynically.

Winston nodded compliantly at the ad and made sure his face registered no disapproval. He was less able to control his mind. It flashed back in time to his excitement the first time he was old enough to vote, in the 2004 presidential race. He had campaigned for President George O. Blush in that hotly-contested race, becoming what Russ Limetoff, on his widely syndicated conservative radio show, called "a loyal GOB-ber willing to stand up for its leader in Time of War." Winston thought nostalgically of that year's robust debate, the vigorous campaigning. But despite his support of the Administration, he was disappointed with the tactics it used to secure its lock on power after its narrow 2004 reelection victory.

The power consolidation had begun in 2005, soon after Andrew Scaria was made Chief Justice of the Supreme Court. A precedent-setting Supreme Court ruling late that year established the government's unrestricted right to "selective searches," of specific types of citizens, in Time of War. Then, in 2006, the President and the Nationalist-majority congress narrowly pushed through the strictest rewriting of the federal drug laws in history. A few moderate Nationalist Senators explained to a concerned public that the increased federal penalties for marijuana use would rarely be used, but that it would be a necessary tool in the government's terrorist-fighting arsenal.

Homeland Security General Bashcrost saw it differently. On Election Day, 2006, as Americans were heading to the polls for the federal midterm election, the General launched *Operation Clean Sweep*. In African-American, Hispanic, and liberal-leaning neighborhoods across the country, people arriving at their polling places were taken aside for instantaneous hair tests. With the backing of the military and national guard, the largest police action in American history resulted in the arrest and automatic conviction of millions of would-be voters whose hair tested positive for marijuana residue from the past three months. The new mandatory sentence was ten years in privatized prison labor camps, with a felony conviction that prevented the violators from ever voting again.

With millions of Democratic Party-leaning voters out of the picture, the Nationalists swept the midterm elections of 2006. Next came the complex passage of a constitutional amendment eliminating presidential term limits "in Time of War," which was necessary to allow President George O. Blush to run for a third term. The President's landslide reelection in 2008 brought with it an overwhelming Nationalist majority in Congress, and "subversive" opposition parties were soon outlawed.

Perhaps, Winston wondered, thinking of his mother's critique, the political pendulum had swung too far to the right. Was dissent really so harmful?

Winston shifted on the subway bench and stretched his neck. He was uncomfortable with his own cynicism and was beginning to feel like a defeatist "whiner." He realized that he was reacting emotionally to Swan's decision to kill the *1984* project. He reminded himself that he still had a high-paying, prestigious job, a beautiful penthouse, a sexy girlfriend. He didn't want to wallow in self-pity. He would try to get Neil Swan to reconsider, perhaps rename the Ministry of Truth in his movie something clever, like the Ministry of Islamic Truth. If the appeal failed, Winston promised himself, he would get over it quickly, and get on with his life.

DAWN BLAIR

Four

The ear-splitting screech of the subway pulling into the 14th Street station interrupted Winston's thoughts. He looked at the billboard across from him, and noticed that one of his long public service ads was beginning.

The commercial showed a Caucasian man, middle-aged and bearded, an anarchist type with a video camera hidden in his eye-glasses, surveying a crowded train station and its security gate. The next image was the man reviewing the video of the train station from a bomb-making den filled with Arab terrorists. "Subversive?" the soundtrack asked ominously. "Patriotic Citizens have a legal and moral obligation to be vigilant. Help us help you by protecting God's United States from those who would terrorize and enslave us. Call 811." The numbers flashed huge across the screen, then the image shifted to a businesswoman in the subway station dialing 811 on her digital phone. A second later, a squad of enormous Homeland Security troopers were pictured arresting the suspicious man, forcing him into a full-body incarceration suit, then wheeling him away, while the soundtrack sternly advised, "Homeland Security will be there in moments. **Better safe and free than sorry™.**"

Winston had created that trademark, and had Party lawyers register it, like all the patriotic slogans, for the Nationalist Party. The federal government got public service airtime for free, but it paid a royalty to the Party every time one of its slogans was used. Although less than one percent of the royalties trickled down from the top Party brass to a creator at Winston's level, the ads were in continuous rotation all over the country. Winston hoped to collect "Party Consulting Fees" from his slogans for the rest of his life.

A vagrant entered the car with the loud clanging of coins. The man, not much older than Winston, was covered in rags, with a layer of black soot embedded in his skin. He smelled like a garbage Dumpster, and wore an enormous pulsing red "S" pendant around his neck.

"Please help the homeless and destitute," the man begged, surprisingly well spoken, as he shook the few coins in his cup. "I was branded a Subversive and fired from my job for buying a banned book three years ago. Been looking for work ever since. Ran out of savings, no medical benefits, lost our apartment, wife is sick. Two little kids, and none of us eligible for health services or welfare 'cause of this S. We're sleepin' out on the streets of the Bed-Stuy ghetto, please, we have nowhere to turn . . ."

Winston cursed himself for paying attention to the man, and quickly turned back around. He worried about the cameras behind the video billboard. Everyone knew that it was illegal to panhandle and jeopardize security in the subway. Winston had heard of Homeland Security agents going undercover as lawbreakers to flush out non-vigilant citizens. He was a Patriotic Citizen, a Party member. His connections would eventually get him released from any such sweep, but his complacency in the face of lawbreaking would go on his record. It might even affect his career.

Winston fingered his phone. All he needed to do was hold it

up, hit record, and dial 811. He would just be doing his duty.

But the consequences for the man would be severe. A prison labor camp. A starving family left behind. Winston's finger froze. He worked hard to keep his eyes fixed on a video billboard, wishing that he hadn't turned to look at the beggar. He might argue that he was focusing on his work, that he needed to watch the next commercial for a report on viewer response.

It was a simple billboard, a quick text-only message that ended with a close-up of the President. It had come straight from Washington, with no need for input from Winston's team, except for the color of the gigantic digital words. Winston watched them flash through. "The Subversives and Treasoncrats had called it a system of checks and balances . . . a system in which Almighty God Himself was held in check by left-wing atheists . . . Finally we have a Leader who trusts in God . . . And a country that trusts that Leader . . . God Bless President George O. Blush!"

Winston nodded his head in silent agreement, listening intently to the beggar, who had stopped just a few feet past him and was repeating his plea for assistance. Winston lifted his phone out of its holder with a sweaty hand.

Winston turned back around, ready to report the offender. He noticed that a stocky man in a sleeveless tee shirt across the aisle was already holding his phone high to record and transmit the offense. He nodded his encouragement for the surveillance cameras, but felt relieved as he put his own phone back.

An older woman with a flowery scarf, seated just a few feet from where Winston was standing, dropped a handful of coins into the man's cup, defiant of the recordings that were taking place. The man reporting the crime glared at her.

The security call worked quickly and efficiently. As the train pulled slowly into the 42nd Street station, two hulking Homeland Security troopers in riot gear were already on the platform. The doors stayed shut until the troopers got in position, then opened. The vagrant stumbled desperately over people to evade the troopers, but they had split up, entering through two doors, and quickly closed in on him. One of the troopers slammed a steel black-jack into the man's knee, shattering it with a sickening thud. Tears of pain streamed from the beggar's eyes as he fell to the ground. He pleaded with the passengers around him for help, but they quickly moved away, not daring to interfere or question the troopers, whose faces were masked by dark, impenetrable face shields.

Winston stared intently at the video billboards, listening to the cries of pain and the sound of the man's body being dragged onto the platform. He watched from the corner of his eye as the troopers lifted the vagrant into a waiting incarceration suit. The frantic pleas for help became louder and shriller for an instant, then were muffled into silence as a huge hood was zipped shut over his face.

As the train pulled out, Winston noticed that the older woman with the colorful scarf was looking angrily at the man who had reported the beggar. The woman was about sixty-five, and a small wooden cross hung from her neck. She reminded Winston of his mother.

"What—what are you staring at?" the stocky man in the tee shirt demanded. "You should be thanking me. A terrorist could use that bum routine to spread chemical weapons, and we'd never know it!"

"Have you no sense of decency?" the woman responded, her voice surprisingly strong, speaking not just to the man but to everyone on the train.

She seemed fearless. Winston remembered, with a sense of shame, how he had criticized his mother, before blocking her calls and e-mails from her refuge in Costa Rica. He had been deter-mined not to let his career be tainted by contact with her. "You disguise your weakness as empathy," he had said, borrowing a slo-gan from Russ Limetoff's radio show. "And your ignorance of the real world masquerades as religious compassion while killers roam free!"

The train slowed as it arrived at the Columbus Circle station. Winston lined up at the subway door. "Better safe and free than sorry!" the stocky man yelled at the defiant woman.

Winston smiled approvingly for the surveillance cameras, then left the train.

He rode an escalator to the security lobby of the VALUED Entertainment building, a massive modern skyscraper that had originally been built to house the headquarters of AOL Time Warner. VALUED was the result of the mergers of conglomerates once called Viacom, AOL Time Warner, Liberty, Universal, E Entertainment, and Disney. The company produced all of the country's entertainment content, and had shut down all its news networks in compliance with Homeland Security orders. As long as it submitted all material to the F.C.C. Compliance Department for prior approval, VALUED Entertainment's monopoly on the market guaranteed an impressive profit margin.

Winston filed through the building's security checkpoints thinking about what the man had shouted, about the beggar, about his movie project, and about freedom. The *1984* remake was a potentially profitable and patriotic project that slammed only America's enemies. Winston's company, VALUED Entertainment, had approved and budgeted the project internally. They had even scheduled its sale on Interactive Pay-Per-View before the end of the year. The company's bean-counters had estimated that *1984* could net the company a profit of more than twenty million dollars. So why weren't they free to make it?

Winston immediately decided against framing his argument to Susan Giccanti this way. It was too contrarian, and he did not want the powerful Executive Vice President in charge of VALUED's TV films thinking he was a Subversive sympathizer. No, he thought, as the elevator sped him quickly upward, he would need a much better argument than that to sway Susan— provided he managed to see her.

The least she could do, Winston thought, is give me a fair

hearing. After all, the group that produced Homeland Security public service ads—the division Winston ran—brought in more government revenue than any other commercial production division. In addition to an annual salary exceeding one million dollars, Winston's excellent relationship with Neil Swan allowed him to occasionally lobby the government's powerful head of Compliance about other large VALUED projects, including a few from Susan Giccanti's division. The time had come, Winston thought, to ask Susan to return the favor and provide corporate support for something important to him.

Swan was not beyond reconsidering decisions, Winston would argue. It had happened before, when Swan had ordered Winston to change an ad, and the change hadn't worked out. Winston showed the revised ad with Swan's changes, along with the version he preferred. Swan had agreed that Winston was right, reversed his decision, and even praised Winston's original version.

Winston filed past cubicles of workers and signaled for his assistant to bring him a cup of coffee. He entered his spacious office. Floor to ceiling windows offered a breathtaking view of Central Park sixty-five stories below. Sipping his dark roast, Winston ordered his computer system to move the video monitor to conference position, and told it to dial Susan Giccanti's assistant.

Danielle looked annoyed. "Face time today will be impossible."

"Five minutes," Winston replied, with a friendly smile, trying his best to charm her. "I'll be in and out in five minutes."

"She's booked solid. Best she *might* do today is a two minute call, and that's still a big *might*."

"C'mon Danielle, you can do better than that . . ."

Susan's assistant shook her head. "Will you be there for a call within the next hour or not? That's the only time she might have free."

Winston nodded and hung up. His head throbbed. A video call would not be optimal. He would be asking Susan to expend a lot of personal capital on his behalf. He considered whether he should just park himself outside her office and catch her between meetings, but decided that would make him appear too desperate.

Winston sprawled across his office couch, stretched out, and barked an order to his office computer, "Organizer, move the screen to the south wall and play messages."

Winston's magnetized flat video screen moved across the wall into a position where he could watch it from the couch. The image of his girlfriend Lilly, just waking up, appeared on the screen, wearing a maroon-colored silk slip and nothing else. She was a striking Chinese-American dancer with a slight, sensual figure. She pouted seductively at the telephone camera, "I'm sorry I woke up so late, Winny. I wanted to shower together, but I was sooooo tired." She yawned. "I woke up wondering how you and the big *1984* meetings were going. I just know this is going to be your greatest project ever! My dance company has rehearsal most of the afternoon, but I'll be home by six o'clock to cook dinner for our celebration date!"

The message only upset Winston more. He had never felt like such a failure. He didn't care what the office surveillance camera showed—he had a right to be disappointed. Too depressed to move, he lay on the couch for an hour, staring at the ceiling. Finally, he sat down at his desk and told his computer to search for travel packages to Las Vegas.

The attractions all seemed tedious and contrived. All he really wanted to do, he thought, was make his film. He pulled a paper notepad out of his desk and jotted down some talking points for his conversation with Susan, not wanting to leave a record of them on his organizer tablet.

Danielle buzzed him. "Susan's picking up. She has two minutes."

Winston tried to ignore the pain in the back of his head as he told his computer to move his video screen higher on the wall for the call.

Susan appeared, looking harried. She was not much older than Winston, a thirty-something careerist with enormous power and a salary to match. She wore a stylish pants suit with a jacket tight enough to reveal her thin, muscular form. She was well-toned, well-tanned, well-coiffed, well-manicured, and not so well-mannered, but that came with the territory.

"Whassup?" she demanded.

"I know that Neil Swan called you. Would you consider an appeal?"

"Winston, what planet have you been on? When Neil Swan himself says D.B.A., it means D.B.A. This is not the sort of decision you can appeal."

"You've got juice around here, Susan. Couldn't you take it upstairs to corporate? This means a lot to—"

Susan made no attempt to disguise her impatience. "Waste of time, and I don't have any to waste. Danielle," she yelled out her door, while pulling Winston's script off a shelf and plopping it on her desk like a blunt weapon. "Get this shredded by the time I get back from my next meeting. Delete all associated files and communications."

Susan returned her attention to Winston. He swore he could detect a smug look on her face, like she had just won something. The bitch. His head throbbed even more. "Listen, Winston, take a vacation, come back refreshed. I hear Las Vegas has a new Mount Everest location."

"What do you want me to do with—"

"Hell-lo. What did I just do? Shred the scripts, shred the books, delete all references. Then have a ni-ice vacation. Gotta go!"

Susan disappeared from the screen.

Winston felt beaten down. It was over. He dropped all the drafts of his script and copies of the book into his super-shredder and left the office, his head feeling like a pulsing sack of lead between his shoulders.

All Winston could think of was heading home and going to bed. He grabbed his organizer, and made a quick check of his mail. His department head had sent a v-mail confirming that his three week vacation had been approved. Attached was a coupon offering special Las Vegas discounts to VALUED Entertainment executives.

FIVE

Although it was only three o'clock, Winston headed downstairs for the subway home. His headache was compounded by the sound of rowdy school kids rushing around the station.

Boarding a downtown train, he hoped that the video billboards would distract him. He was pleased to see an image of a man looking as beaten down as he was. "Stressed out?" the voiceover and textual caption beneath the image asked. "Boss got you down? Worried about the next terrorist attack? You deserve some happiness tonight!" The unhappy man was shown transported to a park, running after a beautiful woman, both of them shrieking with pleasure. "Wellness Pharmaceuticals now offers three flavors of Happiness Cocktails™: Amour™, Silly™, and Carefree™. What kind of happiness do you want tonight?" The image of the euphoric couple was replaced by that of a medical expert in a white laboratory coat. "Remember," he advised, "Those with insurance have a Constitutional Right to pharmacological happiness! And your HMO must pay! Come in to your nearest pharmacy for a free mental well-being test, or tell your doctor that you deserve a little Happiness™."

That ad could not have come at a better time, Winston thought. He would stop at the pharmacy next to the West 4th Street subway exit. It was right on the way home. He wondered what the test would say. Of course he needed a Happiness Cocktail. Which flavor did he feel like?

The next commercial, a public service announcement for Medicare, was not nearly as uplifting. It showed a concerned, middle class couple visiting a comatose man in a hospital bed. "The doctor said that another operation might keep your dad alive for one more month," the woman said. "But," the husband replied, "he's well beyond his one thousand dollar annual maximum Medicare reimbursement. It would mean taking out a second mortgage on the house—and never taking a vacation again." The camera zoomed in on the comatose father, and the words, "1 month = $200,000" appeared across his face. A very gentle off-screen voice concluded, "Nobody lives forever. Expiration is an honorable choice—and it's fully covered by Medicare if you act early."

Winston found the subject to be a downer. He fleetingly wondered how affluent his country really was when the federal budget could not pay for what Russ Limetoff called "the socialist-style programs of yesteryear," like Medicare and Social Security.

Winston adjusted his face for the camera behind the billboard. He didn't want to look as though it was the ad that had upset him. Biometric facial patterns were constantly assessed by the video monitoring computer system, and the last thing he wanted was a late-night visit by Homeland Security goons to discuss his patriotism. He looked down and returned to thinking about what flavor of cocktail he wanted for the evening.

When Winston arrived at the pharmacy, there were only two people ahead of him at the Happiness Cocktail kiosk. He stood a polite distance back until it was his turn, then stuck his finger into the testing chamber. The device collected dead skin cells, accessed his identity and medical records, then made some kind of proprietary assessment of his DNA. For a few seconds Winston worried whether the test might conclude that he did not need a Happiness Cocktail. Of course he needed one. The most important project of his life had just been cancelled, he had every reason to be upset! And as the flashing sign above the kiosk reminded him, he had a constitutional right to pharmacological happiness.

The kiosk's video screen pulsed with a green light approval, and the message, "Winston Smith: Wellness Pharmaceuticals has determined that **you deserve a little happiness!**™ Just tell us which flavor of Happiness Cocktail™ you want, and your prescription will be waiting at the pharmacist's counter. And thanks to the Nationalist Party, your insurance now covers 100% of the cost of your happiness."

Winston selected two doses of "Amour." He had been so anxious about his *1984* project that he and Lilly had not had sex in more than three weeks, by far the longest period since she moved in eight months earlier.

By the time he arrived at the pharmacist's counter, his Happiness Cocktail was waiting for him. He ignored the numerous warnings on the bag about potential side effects, signed the requisite legal liability release, and hurried out.

As he passed back by the Happiness Cocktail kiosk, six anxious people were in line. Winston noticed that every person, like him, headed straight for the pharmacist's counter right after their test. He wondered whether anyone ever really failed the kiosk's "test," or whether happiness had become, in effect, a new entitlement program for the quarter of the American population who had health insurance.

Well, he thought, as he headed home, better a thousand nights of lust and laughter than keeping some comatose granddaddy alive an extra month in a hospital bed.

Winston hurried through the security checkpoint in the ornate lobby of One Fifth Avenue and headed home to the luxurious two bedroom apartment he had owned for the past few years. Upstairs, he ordered sushi to be delivered, lowered the shades, set out candles and put on soothing music. Then he turned the video display and volume of his Interactive TV down as far as it would go, so it would only disturb them if there was a terrorist emergency or important government announcement. Swallowing one dose of "Amour," he set Lilly's pill out on the table next to a candle, and drew a hot bath.

By the time Lilly arrived, he was in a much better mood. At first she complained that he had not waited for her before he took his cocktail. Laughing, Winston explained that his project had been killed and he just couldn't wait for his happiness. Then he dropped an "Amour" pill into her mouth with his tongue.

Before long they were laughing hysterically and kissing passionately on the living room floor. They made love before dinner, starting on the floor and pushing up to the couch until they were half buried within the cushions.

Ravenous, they broke for a candlelight dinner. Winston reminisced about his pot-smoking days in college, about how much fun he used to have staying up late with his pals bullshitting the night away, and running around the city doing crazy things. "Too bad it's gotten so illegal and we can't do that anymore," he lamented. "I haven't had a joint since my senior year. It was as good—okay, almost as good—as a Happiness Cocktail."

"It's legal in Europe," Lilly laughed, suddenly feeling hot and pulling her silk negligee off. "Why don't you go to Europe and light up a big one for both of us!"

"That's a great idea," Winston said, feeling a growing urge in his groin. "And I'm supposed to take a three week vacation, starting tomorrow."

"Oh—I've got to work. I would miss you, but—why don't you just head out to Las Vegas? I hear they've got a new—"

"Fuck Las Vegas!" Winston screamed jubilantly. "There are still direct flights to England. I'm going to London to get stoned!"

Winston sprung up and tried to grab Lilly. She ran playfully into the bedroom, then jumped on him when he followed her. She was strong, and enjoyed their wrestling matches, but they both broke down in minutes, and resumed their wild lovemaking long into the night.

Six

Winston was in the airplane lavatory when the pilot announced the beginning of their descent into Heathrow Airport. It was his eighth visit to the toilet since the overnight flight had left New York. His diarrhea was relentless.

More than thirty hours had passed since he and Lilly had taken their Happiness Cocktail "Amour" pills, but the nasty side effects kept coming. Besides the constant diarrhea, there had been an endless stream of painful vomit, which only subsided when there was nothing left in his belly to hurl. He also felt pain in his joints, though not as badly as Lilly, who was still bed-ridden when he left their apartment the previous afternoon.

Winston stumbled back from the toilet, relieved he had an aisle seat. He realized that he stank, and looked straight down to avoid the eyes of the people in the seats nearby. Had they ever taken a Happiness Cocktail, he wondered? There was nothing like it for sex, but he could see why it was a drug that few people indulged in every day. He worried for a moment about the longer-term side effects, shuddered, and was glad that he hadn't looked too carefully at the packaging. He had enough to worry about, with the crushing of his aspiration to become a feature-length film producer.

Winston looked out at the wet runway as the plane landed. He had not been in London since he spent a semester there during his junior year at Columbia University, ten years earlier. The sky was as gray and dreary as he remembered it, and the drizzle was steady. He was glad that God's United States still permitted direct flights from New York. Despite the open antagonism between the two governments, they were not at war, and still retained diplomatic relations.

The security force at Heathrow's immigration checkpoint was as large as New York's, Winston noted, although not nearly as well armed. He waited an hour to reach an inspection booth, where his passport, with his DNA code embedded on a magnetic strip, was checked against a snippet of hair that an immigration agent clipped from his head.

Winston sprinted to the toilet the moment he got through the exit and barely made it. On the morning after he and Lilly took their Happiness Cocktail, he had received an automated video call from Wellness Pharmaceuticals, offering additional drugs to counter the side effects of the Happiness Cocktail. They came with immediate delivery from the nearest pharmacy. But, unlike the Happiness drug itself, which was guaranteed by the revised Constitution to be free for those with health insurance, drugs for treating side effects were expensive, and uninsured. By the time he and Lilly got the automated call, they didn't care how much it cost to order two forty-pill treatments of both "Get On With It™", and "Feel Right Again™."

Winston went to a water fountain and took one of each pill, wondering if Lilly had managed to get out of bed yet.

Heathrow Airport was bustling, with more people from

developing countries than Winston had ever seen in American airports. He stopped at a cash machine to withdraw Euros, then boarded a British Rail train to the city.

As the train moved out, Winston was surprised at how the area around Heathrow had been transformed. Refugee and internment camps surrounded the airport for miles in every direction. Some were drab, box-like structures, encircled by high fences topped with razor wire. Others were teeming villages dotted with large institutional tents bearing Red Cross and Red Crescent symbols, discreet electrical fences marking their perimeters.

A well-dressed businessman sat across from him doing a crossword puzzle. Winston hoped that he didn't smell too bad. The man dropped his pen on the floor, apologized, and picked it up from the ground next to Winston's shoe.

Winston was glad the man didn't try to make conversation. He didn't have the energy to defend his country's foreign policy to a stranger. He thought about how much the world had changed in the decade since he had been a college student spending a semester in London. Back then, Tony Fair's England was an ally in the Iraqi War. Soon after Fair was voted out of office, the United Kingdom joined the European Community, which unanimously refused to support America's bloody occupation of Iraq. After the biological terrorist attacks of "Dirty Friday" and the subsequent stock market crash, America brought its War on Terror to Iran, Syria, Pakistan, and eventually Egypt and Indonesia. England joined the E.C. nations and most of the member states of the United Nations in offering support for the battle against Al-Qaeda, but condemning the ever-spreading war. America responded by booting the U.N. out of the country and withdrawing its membership.

Winston tried to put a number to the camps that were visible from the train, in what he had remembered as an area of farms and light industry. He lost count at sixty, and he was only heading in a single direction. He vaguely recalled hearing something about refugees flooding into the European Community from embattled countries, but he had never realized the scale of the problem. There must have been hundreds of thousands of refugees seeking asylum, he thought.

At London's Paddington Station, Paul Goode was waiting on the train platform. Tall, lanky and casually dressed, Paul looked barely older than during their college days. They had shared an apartment for just one semester, but Paul became the only friend from his semester abroad that Winston stayed in touch with. Winston thought of him as one of the most sensible people he had ever met—despite his left-wing politics.

Paul greeted Winston with a hug. "You look like shit," Paul grinned, then helped wheel Winston's bag out to the parking lot.

Winston told him about his Happiness Cocktail hangover, then started the story about how his *1984* project had been killed. Paul listened, not saying much, until they reached the car, an old Peugeot. After loading the bags in, Paul took a small device from his pocket, pressed a switch, and started patting Winston down.

"Talk to any strangers on the way from the airport?" Paul asked, suddenly serious.

"Nope. Just daydreamed out the window, amazed at all the refugee camps that have sprouted up all over. What're you doing with a de-bugging wand anyway?"

The device in Paul's hand beeped frantically as Paul got to Winston's shoes. Paul swept the side of a shoe with a piece of tape, picking off a few dot-sized transmitters, and stuck the tape to the curb. He re-checked Winston. There was no more beeping.

"You didn't tell me about someone licking your boots, you kinky boy. Shall we head on?"

As Paul drove them from the station, Winston tried thinking about his trip. "I guess there was some business guy sitting near me on the train who dropped a pen near my feet. But I can't imagine why British Intelligence would be interested in what I have to say."

"British Intelligence wouldn't be interested in what you have to say," Paul theorized. "They rarely track Americans. But the C.I.A. has so many agents in Europe that it rarely knows what to do with them all. And there aren't nearly as many Yanks traveling abroad as when we were in school."

Winston looked at his watch and smiled. "It took eleven minutes into my visit for the paranoid delusions to start. Are we working toward some sort of record here?"

Paul laughed heartily at himself, one of the finest traits of the English, Winston thought. But Paul was never one to change his opinion easily. "Somebody wanted to bug your visit here. Could it be that your esteemed government doesn't trust you anymore?"

Winston looked out the window and tried to relax. The nausea rose yet again in his stomach. "I can't believe they killed my fucken project," he said. "Now it's back to propaganda videos for the information-starved masses."

Paul looked at him thoughtfully and raised an eyebrow. "How many years have you been doing that?"

"Eight—but who's counting?"

Paul shook his head. "I imagine you are. As you should be."

"I'm here to unwind, put it behind me, so I can head back and start fresh."

"Oh, so that's why you chose London in March—the holiday weather?"

"I wanted to see my old buddy. It's been ages, Paul, and I miss you, and, yeah, believe it or not, I miss London."

"The world beacon of democracy and human rights."

"I thought that was our country," Winston joked.

"You can't be serious, Winston. You don't really believe all that propaganda you make, do you? I mean, it's a living, but you do know the difference between truth and the lies that pay your bills?"

Winston smiled. It was like old times. "Your world view starts and ends with hating America, Paul. What'd we ever do to this country, besides save its ass in World War II?"

Paul shook his head and drove for a while. "Do you ever go to the foreign media websites, or watch BBC World Service anymore? You used to love it when you lived here, and I recall you watching the BBC when I visited you in New York."

Winston gazed out the window. "Promise that you will never ask me a question like that over the phone or v-mail or e-mail. Never."

"I promise."

"Just asking me that question could bring heat down on me. The answer is no, Paul, every piece of media we receive is monitored, and all international media are banned for anyone except those wishing to be labeled 'Subversive' for the rest of their lives. So since I am one of those superstitious people who somehow believes that my livelihood improves when I have a job, as opposed to spending my life in a prison labor camp or filthy ghetto, I'll get my news where the rest of my country—"

Suddenly, Paul's car, which had been winding its way through traffic, screeched to a halt as a ragged, wild-haired maniac swinging a long machete jumped onto the hood.

"Outta the cahr, outta the cahr," he yelled, swatting the side of the machete against the windshield.

Another man, his face shrouded in a hood, rushed to Paul's door and tried to open it, but it had been locked. He jammed a bony, dirty hand into the top of the slightly opened window and tugged at it. "Eee said outta the fucken car or we'll cut your fucken throats. It's our car now, you fucken prigs!"

Paul grabbed a stun gun from beneath his seat. Winston was surprised at how quickly he moved. As the carjacker outside tugged Paul's window loose, Paul shot him with an electronic stun blast.

The carjacker's body trembled, then fell to the ground, paralyzed. The assailant on the hood waving a machete jumped off the car and rushed the broken window. Paul shot him, as well, and he fell to the ground.

"Poor buggers," Paul said, doing his best to place the dislocated window back into its frame.

"Poor buggers?" Winston protested. "They tried to steal your car. Who knows what they would have done to us!"

Paul resumed the drive, calmly, as though nothing had happened. "I suppose you think I should have shot them dead?" he said.

"Why not? Their just rewards. But you don't see that in Manhattan."

"Of course not, you've got all your poor in that ghetto in Brooklyn, or locked away in prison labor camps, slaving away for Nationalist Party cronies. The last Amnesty report I read counted twenty million imprisoned—more than every other country in the world put together."

"Better than leaving them around to carjack everyone else. Anyway, what do you know about our country?" Winston laughed. "They probably wouldn't even let you in."

"Right on that score, Winston. Which is why you have to come here to receive your de-brainwashing."

They both laughed, Winston a bit nervously. Paul had only gotten more radical since they last talked politics on the phone. That was four years ago, before Patriot Act VI outlawed subversive subject matter on international calls.

Everyone knew that all telecommunications were monitored, so Winston had put a stop to their political phone chats. There were plenty of other subjects for them to talk about. Paul's knowledge of Orwell had provided Winston with helpful insight as he embarked on the *1984* project. He enjoyed paying his old friend consulting fees, and made sure that all interpretation was limited to the book itself, and not any left-wing assessments of American foreign policy.

"I've still got copies of the scripts," Paul offered, seeming to read Winston's mind.

"I was ordered to shred all mine," Winston shook his head, feeling queasy at the memory. At the same time, he felt something else, a sense of excitement that a copy of his screenplay still existed. It was right there in London, at the place he was going to. Every trace of it at his office and home had been shredded, deleted, disappeared. But it still existed.

"It's a good adaptation, Winston. You brought it right into the modern world, thirty years later."

"Yeah, that and ten bucks will get me a subway ride." Winston found himself yelling, unable to muffle his outrage. "Our newly-renamed Ministry of Truth killed the project. No appeals. It will never be aired."

"Never in your country, that's for sure, at least not legally. But there could be some interest here."

"The BBC?"

Paul arched an eyebrow. "I approached the head of the original film department. They've been planning a '*1984* Thirty Years Later' adaptation, but don't have a script they like. They're looking to replace the writer. His screenplay's not as good as yours, but there is one big difference."

"What's that?"

"It's set in Washington D.C., not Tehran. And the authoritarian government is yours."

Seven

I t took Winston most of the week to get adjusted to life at Paul's place. When he first arrived at the long, bookcase-lined apartment, he was exhausted from both the sickening side effects of the Happiness Cocktail and the sleepless flight from New York. He slept for a day and a night, a twenty-hour marathon interrupted only by trips to the toilet.

The next morning, Winston joined Paul for tea and met Masashi, Paul's Japanese lover and domestic partner. Homosexual behavior had been outlawed in God's United States under Patriot Act VI, resulting in a mass exodus of gays and lesbians to the European Community and Canada. Gay marriage, Winston learned, was now legal in both those places.

He was surprised by how quickly he felt comfortable with the arrangement. Masashi, a tall, well-mannered chef at a Japanese restaurant, made him ginger tea and an aromatherapy cure. These, along with home-cooked meals, worked far more effectively than the drugs Winston had brought for relief from the side effects of his Happiness Cocktail. Masashi seemed to radiate a warm tranquility. He had decorated the flat in a simple Japanese style, except for the huge common table and randomly collected chairs that filled the spacious dining room.

Paul was happier than Winston recalled from their college days, and far busier. His apartment was a crossroads for London activists. There were Labour Party politicos, dreadlocked anarchists, shaven-headed Buddhists, radical lay Catholics, human rights activists, transgender activists, animal rights activists. They seemed to come from every continent, and were of all different ages and backgrounds. They arrived with flyers, posters, digital communicators. They wrote, they talked, they sipped tea, they drafted posters and produced v-mail and e-mail campaigns. When Paul was off working at the BBC, Masashi hosted the endless stream of visitors. When Masashi and Paul were both at work, a few of them even had keys to the place. They let themselves in and made themselves at home.

Winston was shocked by how freely the activists operated, how they were allowed to keep their jobs, even to work for the government. Concerned that the wrong association could damage his standing with the Party, Winston at first tried to keep his distance. But Paul's flat, up four flights of stairs in an old townhouse, was not that big, and it was hard to avoid them. Winston's resolve to avoid them lasted two days. They were, after all, the ones who brought the hash oil, and that was part of his reason for being there.

Gone were the smoky, tobacco-mixed joints of Winston's college days. Hash was legal in the European Community, and it came in many edible forms, including oil. A few of Paul's friends carried it in small jars. It looked like olive oil, and they liked to spread it on crackers, with peanut butter, for what they called an "enriched snack."

One enriched cracker, on his third day at Paul's, was all it took loosen Winston up. He became far more comfortable with the noisy activists than before. In fact, he had little desire to do anything but sit at the dining room table and snack while debating international politics and ethics with all comers. For a short while, he stuck up for some of the policies of the Blush administration. Then he found himself laughing at some of his own rhetoric. By the time Paul got home from work, a bald Vietnamese Buddhist monk named Thich was showing archived video of Egyptian civilians crippled in Predator drone attacks, and Winston was in a listening mode.

Thich stayed for dinner. Before eating, he asked the others to join him in a prayer for world peace and reduced suffering. Winston went along with it, but was unconvinced.

"When does peace become appeasement?" he challenged, just as they started eating. "Sometimes war is necessary to protect lives, to stop threats before they happen—to reduce suffering and preserve a larger peace."

"The only way to peace is through peace," Thich stated calmly.

Paul was more confrontational, although debate did not slow down his appetite. "Pre-emptive, unilateral war is just another name for international terror," he said, between bites. "If you think the reason your country has been at war since 2001 is to protect American lives, you need to re-read *1984*."

"But Paul," Masashi protested, "they burned all his copies."

Thich laughed with the others, then said to Winston. "You are the first American I have spoken with in years. Why don't you join Paul and Masashi the next time they visit me at work? You could see the other face of your country's wars."

"Which face is that?"

"The human face," Thich replied. "The one they never show on your television."

"Thich works at a hospital camp for badly injured war refugees," Paul explained. "Masashi and I volunteer there on Saturdays."

"I try to heal the soul," Thich said.

Paul noticed that Winston looked concerned. "Don't worry. You'll come in with us. Your name will never enter a database."

By the time the weekend arrived, Winston's biggest objection to spending the day at a refugee camp was that he would miss arguing with his new activist friends all day. It was like being a student all over again. The arguments got easier as soon as Winston gave up trying to speak for his government. "They spend billions to get their points across," he had yelled. "I'm supposed to be on vacation!"

The refugee camp where Thich worked was one of the hundreds of razor wire-enclosed camps that filled the countryside around Heathrow Airport. Masashi woke up early and prepared sushi to serve to the refugees. Paul drove them to the secure entry area at a hospital rehabilitation camp, where they waited for Thich to sign them in.

"Getting into the camp is easy," Paul explained, as Thich joined them, wearing sandals and an orange robe. Thich brought them to a guard station to sit for their video hologram photo ID card. "It's getting out that could be a problem, if you don't have one of these."

In addition to being the Buddhist chaplain, Thich was the coordinator for the camp's volunteers. He knew everyone, and everyone knew that with hundreds of camps to choose from, volunteers should not be unnecessarily inconvenienced. When Winston gave a phony name for his ID card, the lackadaisical security guard did not even bother checking the name in a database.

The refugee camp was a modular, split-level hospital shaped like a wheel within a wheel, with outdoor recreation and rehab areas between the hub and the outer rim. Thich gave Winston an overview as they walked through the crowded hallways. Two hundred dormitory treatment rooms, each holding eight wounded civilian refugees, sixteen hundred beds in all, consistently full. All the patients had been airlifted in by international assistance groups after being seriously injured by drone attacks, uranium-tipped missiles, napalm cluster bombs, and sensor mines. Buildings were organized by country or tribe, among them Pakistanis, Egyptians, Indonesians, Iranians, Iraqis, Syrians, Colombians, Peruvians.

"But I thought you said these were war refugees?" Winston asked. "America pacified Iran, Iraq and Syria years ago. Those wars are over."

Thich looked to Paul to respond. Debate was not his style. "Just because America has moved on to the next international battlefield doesn't mean that the proxy governments it leaves behind have stopped making war on their own people. Or that the sensor mines, napalm cluster bombs, and depleted uranium shells don't continue to kill and maim civilians. They do."

Winston was skeptical. "And Colombia? Peru? You're going to blame America for that, too? There are no wars in Latin America."

"What do you think the War on Drugs is? Peru and Colombia are at war with themselves, their military and paramilitary killers financed by your so-called anti-drug money. More than twenty thousand killed or disappeared each year. We consider it a war against the poor."

"How is that?"

"The poor are the only casualties. Anyone with money buys enough paramilitary security to stay far from harm."

"And who—who is we? I keep hearing this royal 'we' from you—I can't tell you how annoying—"

"We're here to serve today, not argue," Thich reminded them. "I see you brought Masashi's sushi. A favorite of many patients."

"What about the girl with the . . ." Masashi waved his fingers near his legs. "I promised her that I'd return soon. She ate ten pieces last time."

Thich nodded. They followed him through a maze of hallways. Patients, nurses, doctors, therapists, and volunteers mingled chaotically. Some wore traditional clothing, others wore tee shirts or hospital uniforms. The staff seemed overworked.

Thich led them to a crowded dorm room for eight paraplegic teenaged girls, all orphans. Clothes, movie posters, magazines, and stuffed animals were scattered about, as were artificial legs, crutches, wheelchairs and physical therapy equipment. Thich brought Winston, Paul and Masashi to the window, where he found Anna sitting sadly in a motorized wheelchair, staring outside. Masashi unwrapped the sushi he was carrying in a large bag and set it out carefully on two old wooden trays.

Anna's eyes lit up when she saw Masashi. She was small and thin, with a kind, round face, copper skin, and short black hair. She wore a sleeveless nightshirt. It covered the area where her body ended, just below her hips. One of her arms ended in a stump a few inches past her shoulder.

"Masashi," she cried, delighted, as the volunteers approached. Masashi bent down to hug her, then beckoned to Paul and Winston, who were carrying the cloth-covered sushi trays.

"Take your pick," he said, uncovering the trays and handing her chopsticks.

She picked out a large piece of tuna, put it in her mouth and closed her eyes. "Mmmmm," she said.

"We have a new volunteer this week," Masashi announced.

"American," she said, taking another piece off Winston's tray.

"How can you tell?" Winston asked.

"You feel American. Indonesia full of American soldiers. Friendly to meet. Not friendly at security checkpoint."

"Is that . . . where this happened to you?"

"Uh-uh. That's where they killed brother and mother. No good reason. Said they had report that stolen car goes to checkpoint. Report wrong. They blast family car. Even after they see mistake, they never say they sorry."

Winston could not help but fix his eyes on the mangled stump that had once been her left arm. "I'm . . . I'm sorry," he said.

Anna's face relaxed a little. She nodded, closed her eyes, and put another piece of sushi into her mouth. "Delicious!" she said to Masashi. "Delicious!"

"Anna and her family are Indonesian Buddhists," Paul said.

"Yes," Anna continued. "Mother always said we Buddhist, be careful of Muslim terrorists, stay to your own. But was not terrorists who kill her, who kill brother. Was Americans. With checkpoint. And this," she gestured to her mangled stump and absent legs. "This was drone missile. Cripple me. Kill my father and sister. Americans do this."

"Anna was walking home from school when two Predator drones incorrectly determined that she and everyone around her were escaping targets," Paul explained. "She was one of six survivors. Twenty-three dead, all civilians. Anna survived only because the Red Cross got to her in time."

"Red Cross helps people," Anna said, staring deeply into Winston's eyes. "American army hurts people. Why? Do American people know this?"

Winston hoped somebody would say something. Nobody did. He wished he hadn't agreed to volunteer. Anna's unblinking, accusing eyes stared at him.

"Do we . . . do we Americans know this is happening?" Winston stammered, working hard to access, in his memory, how Bob O'Manley, the articulate Secretary of State, characterized civilian casualties. He remembered, then recited the Party line: "Most people know why our army is in Indonesia, yes: to help the Indonesian people find freedom. But it takes a long time, and we also know that you can't make an omelet without breaking eggs—"

"Eggs!" Anna yelled. Tears rolled down her face. "Do I look like egg to you?"

Winston felt his body shaking. He wanted to disappear. His

eyes darted around, looking for a place to hide. He considered crawling under a bed.

"Is my mother egg?" Anna demanded, the intensity of her voice growing. "Was my brother egg?" she shrieked. "Get out, get out, get out of here, America, killer, killer, killer, killer . . ." Anna collapsed in tears and grief.

Thich put an arm around her. "Paul, please leave the other girls some of that tasty sushi, then take Winston and Masashi to the Peru ward where we are scheduled to deliver lunch. I'll meet you there later." Thich stroked Anna's hair. "We're going to chant and relax for a while."

Nobody spoke as Winston and Masashi followed Paul through the busy corridors to the Peruvian ward. Winston's legs felt heavy. He resolved to escape the moment they passed the main exit.

EIGHT

Winston waited in the parking lot for three hours while Paul and Masashi finished their volunteer service. Anna's pain and his insipid Party-line response played over and over in his mind as he thought about her and his government's wars of occupation.

On the drive back to London, he stared silently out the car window while Paul and Masashi made small talk. He looked into passing cars, wondering about the lives of the other drivers, about the worlds they would be returning home to.

Paul broke the silence ten minutes before they arrived at his flat. "Winston," he said, "I was thinking of meeting a BBC colleague for an Indian lunch buffet tomorrow in Islington. Would you care to join us?"

Winston barely stirred. "Sure. You took me to one of those Sunday buffets when I lived here. Best Indian food I ever had."

"My colleague Amanda is a producer for BBC's original films. She's been working on a thirty-years-later adaptation of

1984, scheduled for release in December. She's the one I spoke with about your screenplay. She's interested in meeting."

"Let's see what happens," Winston replied, despondent.

The next day, Paul took Winston on the Underground to north London's Angel Station, then walked him to a small, colorfully decorated Indian restaurant.

Amanda Patel was waiting for them at a quiet table in the back. She had dark, intelligent eyes, gray-streaked black hair, and a large form that got lost in her bright, free-flowing sari.

Amanda stood up and Paul made the introductions. Then he and Amanda each took out a small sensor wand, and swept one another and their seating area for "American bugs." Finding none, they ordered drinks and selected their food from the buffet table.

As soon as they sat down to eat, Paul placed a sound-cloaking device on the edge of the table, and nodded at Amanda to begin. "A film version of *1984* hasn't been done in thirty years, since . . . well, since 1984, actually," she explained, suddenly all business. "So here we are exactly one generation later, and the BBC has all the financing and scheduling arranged, with a release the week before Christmas. That's eight months from now. Our question is this: How can we best reflect Orwell's totalitarian phenomenon if we set it in 2014?"

"That's exactly the question I set out to answer," Winston replied, between bites. The food was as delicious as he remembered it, and it made him feel a bit better.

"I can understand why this project took on such importance to you, Winston," Amanda continued, her eyes probing Winston's face. "Especially for someone born in 1984, named after the protagonist, by parents who felt very . . . strongly about the subject."

Winston glanced at Paul, and wondered how much Amanda knew about him.

"Amanda and I have worked together since I started with the Beeb, more than eight years ago," Paul explained. "I entrusted her with your version of the script. If anyone can bring this project to life, she can."

Winston felt uncertain. Paul was e-mailed the script because he had been a consultant on it, an Orwell specialist. But who else knew about it? And what would his boss, Neil Swan, do if he knew that Winston had sold the banned script elsewhere?

"Why not use one of your other writers?" Winston asked.

"Your basic characters can use some work," Amanda observed, "But your integration of new technologies is good. What works best is the pervasive sense of hopelessness, poverty, and state terror. Moreover, you have an unusual gift for the language of propaganda."

"Eight years in the field working for the pros, and I guess you learn something," Winston laughed.

"Ah," Amanda agreed, dabbing a napkin to her mouth and setting down her fork. "My sentiment exactly. It is indeed the Blush Administration that manages the most sophisticated propaganda machine the world has ever seen. Not Iran, where you have oddly placed the story. We will set the story in Washington D.C. with a fictionalized government. But with the exception of this difference in venue, your script, quite frankly, is better than the one we developed ourselves."

"But you're talking about a pretty major change," Winston said, his mind racing ahead of the conversation, thinking about what changes he might make to the script were it to be set in Washington.

Amanda was encouraging. "We have a writer who could help you make those changes quickly, but we would still retain some of what you've done. Does your company share the script rights with you?" She stared intently at him. This was the question the meeting hinged on.

Winston considered lying, telling them that VALUED Entertainment shared ownership. That would allow him to back out gracefully. But, he suddenly realized, he didn't want to back out.

"It's my script," Winston replied. "I wrote it on my own time, starting more than two years ago. The F.C.C. has quashed it, and my company has accepted that. There's no place to take it in the States. It'll die on the vine there."

"That would be a shame," Amanda said. "This doesn't have to be a long negotiation. We can pay you two hundred thousand Euros for your script, provided you spend the remaining time you have in London working on the adaptation."

Winston converted the Euros to dollars at one to two. Four hundred thousand dollars, he realized, was a decent offer, especially if they didn't kill him with rewrites. "Once I get back, there's no way I could work on it," Winston said.

"We realize that," Amanda agreed. "That's why we would have one of our writers collaborate with you, get the broad changes, and work on the production until it's done."

"Where—where would you make it?"

"Right here in London. We've got the sets commissioned already. This is happening, Winston, with your script or ours."

"The F.C.C. would never allow it to be distributed in the States."

"If it did, we wouldn't be having this conversation, would we?"

"You could never sell U.S. rights; not for Interactive TV, not box office, not broadcast. You wouldn't make a cent in America."

Amanda shrugged. "We are well aware of all that. Thankfully, there is a marketplace outside God's United States."

"A more urgent question," Paul joined in, "is whether or not you're comfortable doing this, then returning to the States, having defied the Ministry of Truth?"

"So news of the renaming has even reached this far corner," Winston joked.

"Big announcement last week," Amanda replied, laying out a newspaper clipping. "Much fanfare from the newly titled Minister of Truth, Russ Limetoff himself. I imagine *1984* has already been pulled from library shelves and bookstores. What do they do with those books, anyway?"

"The Minister of Truth," Winston repeated, incredulous. "The Minister of Truth. That really takes balls."

"No short supply of those where you come from," Paul agreed. "In all seriousness, Winston," Paul urged. "Please take a day and consider the consequences of this. Your job and perhaps even your life could be imperiled should this become known."

Winston thought about it. "Have you any problem with a pseudonym?" he asked.

"Of course not," Amanda said. "And you need never come into our office. We can communicate exclusively through Paul. I believe he's somewhat familiar with the role of a secret agent."

"A what?" Winston made a mental note to ask Paul what she meant later. "I would prefer anonymity—I don't want to make my boss look bad. This would be . . . our secret."

"Absolutely," Amanda agreed. "So much so that you would have to return here if you ever wanted to view it. We wouldn't even v-mail a copy stateside."

"They do store and review all communication for subversive content," Winston confirmed. "So even the payment would have to be arranged . . ."

"Through me, of course," Paul offered. "Perhaps you could sell me some artwork, some etchings, if you catch my drift?"

"Great minds think alike," Winston agreed.

"So," Amanda concluded, "you can think it over and let Paul know your decision tomorrow morning. Meanwhile, shall we return to the buffet?"

By the time they finished, they had eaten enough for both lunch and dinner. Paul declined Amanda's offer of a ride, as he was determined to keep their meeting as secret as possible. He even waited for her to leave before he and Winston exited.

"Aren't you overdoing this secret agent routine?" Winston asked, as they walked a few blocks to the underground station.

"Just trying to protect an old friend," Paul said. As they approached the station, their path was blocked by a few British police officers, who had just arrived and were in the process of closing the sidewalk and street around the tube entrance.

Sirens announced the arrival of more emergency vehicles.

"You'll need to stand back, sirs," a police officer said, holding out his hands to block the way. "The Angel tube is closed until further notice."

A very loud argument was taking place on the sidewalk just forty feet behind the officer. "Get your fucken hands off me, dickweed, I'm a U.S. Marshal," yelled a broad, thick-necked man in a black leather jacket, as he took powerful, wild swings with a steel blackjack at four cops who were trying to subdue him. He connected with one officer, who hit the sidewalk with a loud thud. "I'm warning you—back the fuck off me or my people will make sure you never work again!" The other officers charged him with clubs, pummeling him until he fell to his knees with a final groan.

Pedestrians lined up behind Paul and Winston, who scanned the scene from behind a fast-growing line of police officers. An ambulance pulled up next to a half dozen police cars, blocking the road. Paul noticed two other officers on the ground, and nearby, an Arabic-looking man, lying dead in a pool of blood that continued to drip from an open wound in his throat. Paul pointed the man out to Winston.

An armored limousine pulled up behind the ambulance, its beacon flashing and siren wailing. A man Winston's age in a well-tailored suit jumped out, followed by three bodyguards. They were met by a phalanx of a dozen British police officers, who formed a human wall around the four men on the ground.

"I am the American consul," the well-dressed man announced. "That man is a Homeland Security Bounty Hunter Marshal on official duty for God's United States. I insist that you release him to my custody immediately."

The British cops angrily stood their ground, carefully watching the bodyguards, whose hands wavered menacingly around their waists. A handful of other heavily armed British officers seemed to arrive out of nowhere, and immediately fixed their weapons on the Americans.

"How dare you block my way?" said the American diplomat. "I demand to speak with your commanding officer immediately."

"Speak with him at Scotland Yard, sir," a silver-haired officer in the middle of the human wall replied. "This man committed cold-blooded murder, then assaulted and injured three of my men. The only place he's going is to jail."

The consul assessed the situation, noting the number of weapons pointed at his men. He signaled to them to stay calm. "That marshal was executing a warrant as part of his official duty as a law enforcement officer of God's United States. Release him immediately!"

"You can kiss my English arse," the British cop snarled.

"I'll have your badge for this," the consul threatened.

The British S.W.A.T. team members kept their weapons fixed as the American diplomat edged back to his car.

"Williams, Torrance—follow this . . . diplomat." With this, the silver-haired British detective spat on the ground, "And make sure he doesn't interfere with our transport."

The confrontation over, Paul and Winston backed out of the growing crowd of spectators to make their way home from a different tube station.

"Cheeky diplomat," Paul commented, as they walked.

"I'm surprised the bounty hunter assaulted your cops," Winston said, startled by what he had seen. "And I . . . I didn't know they worked in foreign countries."

"Your government is a law unto itself. Perhaps you ought to think about applying for asylum, and staying here."

Winston stopped walking and folded his arms, incredulous. "Me—move to London? Now?"

"Just a suggestion. I've a good friend who is an attorney. The U.K. accepts asylum from any Yankee with a reasonable fear of persecution at home. You could stay with Masashi and me until you get sorted out."

"You're crazy," Winston protested. "I've got a girlfriend in

New York, a fantastic job, making serious bucks. I'm a . . . I'm a member of the Nationalist Party, for God's sake. You know what it takes to get to where I am? You should see my fucken penthouse apartment!"

Paul shrugged and they continued walking. "Amanda and I will do our best to conceal your identity, but I cannot guarantee success. Your government pays informants everywhere. I tell you this with some understanding of the Resistance movement."

Winston had been itching to ask about this. "Are you . . . are you . . . ?"

"Are you now or have you ever been a member of the Communist Party?" Paul replied theatrically. "Oh, such a rich history America has. Why don't we shelve that question for now? My answer could end up being burdensome to you. Think of what we've just seen. Then imagine the power your government has if it decides to retaliate against a person when he's not on foreign soil."

"That Arab was probably a terrorist," Winston replied. "I'm a member of the Party in good standing and America is still a free country, isn't it?"

"I know that the Blush government has trademarked the *Freest Country in the World*, but I can't say that the mark is recognized outside God's United States."

"What are you trying to say?" Winston laughed nervously.

"Seriously, Winston, consider asylum or even passing on the project. The BBC can make the movie with or without you. I would . . . I would feel terrible if something happened to you."

"Paul, listen. This is a freelance project that means a lot to me, done in my own time, not even to be aired in the States. I think that I'm standing on pretty solid ground."

"I wish you would think more about it," Paul asked, unusually persistent.

"I can take care of myself," Winston insisted. "You Brits worry about making a great movie."

NINE

The International Arrivals terminal at New York's JFK airport bustled as Winston waited in a long line to get to the Passport Control checkpoint. A sixty-foot banner stretched across the entry area, welcoming visitors with the proclamation: "God's United States: The Freest Country On Earth™."

Smaller signs along pillars advised, "Warning: This is a Technological Dead Zone," but Homeland Security did not rely upon people's good will. A top-secret system that Winston could barely begin to understand blanketed the entry area with electromagnetic waves that neutralized all technology. Even wristwatches stopped keeping time, and needed to be reset once passengers exited the passport control and customs areas.

It took an hour for Winston to get to the front of the Passport Control line, and he was glad that he had advised Lilly not to come to the airport to meet him until an hour after his scheduled arrival. Homeland Security troopers in high black boots and dark glasses directed those at the head of the line to one of a dozen inspection areas. Each area had its own door, sealing it off completely from the gaze of onlookers.

Unable to use his phone, Winston waited impatiently, retracing, in his mind, the past three weeks in London.

Once he'd gotten to writing every day, the time had passed quickly. Changing the protagonist from an Iranian to an American was a major job, even with the writing assistant that Amanda assigned. His deadline, dictated by the date that his office expected him to return, was met by working through the night during bursts of creative energy. He had completed a revised draft. Now his assistant would manage through the BBC rewrites. Winston would never see the script again.

Had he done the right thing, Winston wondered, in continuing work on his *1984* project even after it had been banned by his powerful boss? He reassured himself that Neil Swan was a friend, a mentor. Even if he found out—which was doubtful, since the movie would never air in America and not have his name attached—he might understand.

A digital sign directed Winston to a door. He walked through and was met by an immigration officer, who requested his passport. "Please stand on the red line for a body scan, and look up at a forty-five degree angle to verify identity," the officer instructed in a dull monotone, as he swiped the passport through the computer.

A pleasant woman's voice spoke from the retina scanner. "Welcome back to God's United States, Mr. Winston Smith, National ID #763-83-1293. Was your twenty-day trip to London for business or pleasure?"

"Pleasure," Winston said.

"Voice scan affirmed," the voice concluded.

The immigration official wore decoding glasses that allowed him to read Winston's identity data from the encrypted screen in front of him. He looked up from the screen and sounded unconcerned. "Please follow me to the room immediately on your left for a random Biometric Palm Print test."

The immigration guard ushered Winston through an unmarked door into a tiny room. "Please stand on the red line, place your hand, palm down, into the reader," the guard instructed. "This will just take a minute."

They must be testing a new identity control system, Winston thought, placing his hand flat down on a scanning device that he had never seen before.

The machine scraped off a few dead skin cells, read his DNA, and in two seconds, a mechanical voice asked: "Are you Winston Smith, National ID #763-83-1293?"

"Yes, I am," Winston replied.

Suddenly, a needle shot out from the device and jabbed into his exposed wrist. "Ouch!" Winston yelled, more surprised than hurt. He tried to turn his head to ask the guard what was happening, but his body felt paralyzed. The floor beneath him gave way, and the last thing he could remember before losing consciousness was dropping through a trap door into the unknown.

The chute narrowed, delivering Winston's unconscious body neatly into an open incarceration suit. A robot zipped the hood over his head, pasted a label with Winston's name and ID number on the chest area, and hooked the suit's shoulder rings onto a conveyor belt. The belt carried Winston to a cargo bay, where he joined three dozen other unconscious suspects in the holding belly of a large Homeland Security military helicopter.

Lilly waited at the customs exit door for an hour after the last passenger from the British Airways flight departed. She was not, by nature, a suspicious person, but it had been three hours since Winston's flight landed. She approached the Homeland Security bunker at the customs exit door and stepped up to the information window. A large sign next to it read, "Report Suspicious People Here!"

A microphone extended from the darkened glass of the window. She could not see if anyone was inside or not, but she figured there was nothing to lose by taking hold of the microphone and speaking into it.

"Hi," she said anxiously. "I'm looking for my boyfriend, Winston Smith, who was scheduled to arrive on British Airways Flight 227 a while ago. He knew I would be here, but he never came out of the exit door. Is there another place that he might have exited? Or is there a way I can know if he made it on the plane, or is being detained for any reason?"

"Release the microphone immediately!" a burly voice commanded, through a very loud speaker system. "Be advised that under Section 726 of Patriot Act VI, it is a federal crime to question a representative of Homeland Security about possible proceedings against any individual. Further information about federal protocol and the law concerning such inquiries may be found only through the Homeland Security website, at www.protectingyou.gov."

"But, but—uhh—could you at least tell me if he was on that plane, or whether there's another exit, or—"

"You must remove yourself from this window within the next ten seconds," the man in the booth ordered. "Or you will be arrested for the federal crime of circumvention of national security protocols. This is your only warning, you have four seconds!"

Shocked and frightened, tears streamed down Lilly's face as she backed away from the booth, determined to keep waiting for Winston's arrival.

TEN

Winston had no idea how much time had passed since he had been drugged at the airport. He had experienced a feeling of being moved around for hours within the incarceration suit. He recalled a diaper-like area around his crotch being replaced by men who yelled crude insults that he could only partially make out through the thick hood that kept him in terrible darkness.

Machines and people kept hooking and unhooking the suit that enveloped his body, which hung limp, unable to move. He realized that he could not even scratch his nose, which was itching terribly, and probably dripping all over his face.

Then, quite suddenly, after a great deal of movement, the latch on the security hood attachment was unclipped, the zipper across Winston's shoulders opened, and bright lights blinded him. His name was being yelled out.

"The People versus Winston Smith," he heard, as his eyes focused on a powerfully built, uniformed man, with red, white and blue braids embellishing his broad shoulders.

What time was it, Winston wondered? He still felt groggy, but could now clearly make out his surroundings.

He was in a high security courtroom. A judge in a black robe sat behind an enormous desk. Mounted on the wall behind him were large, framed inscriptions, one on top of another, circling a replica of the Ten Commandments carved in stone. The largest inscription said, **"In The Homeland Security Court, The Presiding Judge Is God!"** Another read, **"In God Lies Freedom, But There is No Freedom From God,"** and under that it, **"In God's United States, We Have No King But Jesus."**

The side wall held the largest American flag Winston had ever seen indoors. Over it, in four-foot high letters, were the words **"One God, One Truth, One Law."**

"Winston Smith!" the judge roared, interrupting Winston's visual inspection of the courtroom. He was a chubby, sullen-faced balding man, who pulled off a pair of wire spectacles and peered accusingly at Winston. Winston's eyes searched for a nameplate, but none existed. "You have been accused," the judge continued loudly, "by the Government of God's United States of the felony crime of subversive behavior, and the felony crime of possessing the illicit drug marijuana in your blood. How do you plead?"

The courtroom was quiet. Winston looked around. There were only himself, the judge, the court officer, and a small, bored-looking dark-suited man. Was that his lawyer?

As he turned to check if anyone was sitting next to or behind him, Winston saw two heavily armed guards, one of whom was attached to his incarceration suit by a chain. They scowled at him.

"You will face forward and pay attention to this court!" yelled the judge. "I am losing my patience here, and you do not want to see what happens, you do not want to fuck with me when that happens. Do you understand?"

Winston nodded nervously. The small man in the dark suit looked down at the floor. Trying to keep his eye respectfully on the judge, Winston prayed that the small man would speak up on his behalf.

"I mean, I may be a wee bit out of shape, and I may not pack the kind of steel you boys do . . ." the judge said, winking at the court officer and the two Homeland Security troopers flanking Winston, "but I can take care of myself, with Smith and Wesson's help." The judge pulled a massive handgun with laser sights out of his robe, and laid it proudly on the table in front of him, like a school kid at show-and-tell. "I may have twenty, okay, thirty years on you boys, but if somebody fucks with me, I will chew their motherfucken head off and spit it into the fucken gutter." He suddenly turned back to Winston. "Am I making myself absolutely clear?

"Yuh—yes . . . yes sir," Winston stammered.

"Now for the last fucken time, Winston Smith, you are charged with subversive behavior and marijuana-in-your-blood possession. How do you plead?"

Winston looked imploringly at the slight man in the suit. The man looked away.

Winston realized that he was on his own. "I—I would like the opportunity to speak with a lawyer, Your Honor?"

The judge dropped his jaw in mock shock. "Ooohh, he'd like the opportunity to speak with a lawyer, wouldn't he." The judge continued in a mocking, high-pitched tone, trying his best to sound like a dainty Southern lady. He stood up and pranced around his chair. "Ah would like dah opptoonitee to speak wuth a lawyer, yoah honor? Ah would like dah opptoonitee to speak wuth a lawyer."

As the court officer and the man in the suit laughed appreciatively, the judge's voice quickly turned severe. "And while we're at it, how about a court stenographer, a video record of these here proceedings, maybe even a court of appeals where this God-loving judge's decisions could be reviewed, condemned and overturned by a bunch of liberal queers! Maybe a 'democratic process' and oversight hearings so that these queers could even challenge Homeland Security department appointees of this special Terrorist and Subversive Court? I suppose that you would like those things too?"

Winston was frozen in place. His legs felt weak, and it was hard work to keep them from collapsing.

"Well, you raghead-lovin' pussyshit, I would like the opportunity to stick my foot up your subversive asshole right now, but I may not get that opportunity, or will I?" The judge smiled at his own cleverness.

Winston shivered with fright and hoped that the judge would not demand a response.

"You fucken better be scared, you little pinko traitor. I got news for you, in case you haven't heard: God's United States is at war, and, thank Jesus in his mercy, my brother in Christ Attorney General John Bashcrost himself appointed me to this court! And there are no appeals to Homeland Security Court proceedings, no fatcat Legal Aid lawyers for raghead-loving devils like you, no Geneee-va fairy convention accords to get lectured about! Blue-blooded American boys are sacrificing their lives in Pakistan and Indonesia at this very moment, so that even a Subversive like you can have the freedom to receive sentencing in a proper court of law. But instead of 'Thank you,' all you can say is 'Ah would like dah opptoonitee to speak wuth a lawyer.'"

"I am sorry, Your Honor."

The judge's face flushed red with anger, his double chin bobbed up and down. "You have insulted the dignity of this here Homeland Security Court in God's United States, and all you can say is that you are sorry? Well, you will be fucken sorry when the People of God's United States finish with you!

"Now let's start again," the judge continued, "and let's get it right this time. The People of the United States accuse you,

Winston Smith, of the felony crime of subversive behavior, first degree, and the felony crime of in-blood marijuana possession. How do you plead?"

"Uhhhh, not guilty, Your Honor, not guilty . . . I ate hash oil in London a few weeks ago, but it's legal there and—"

"I didn't hear what you said there, dopehead? Whuss that you said? Remember, boy, Jesus is listening, Jesus is in this freakin' courtroom, Jesus is our king, and Jesus is going to hear what you are about to say. And as the Lord is my guide, and my witness, let me say here that if you lie to Christ our Almighty, the vengeance of this court will come down upon you and crush you like a flea. **Jeremiah 21:5: 'And I myself will fight against you with an outstretched hand and with a strong arm, even in anger, and in fury, and in great wrath!'** Thus speaketh the Lord our God, Praise God!"

"Praise the Lord!" repeated the court officer enthusiastically.

The judge glared at Winston and waited. "Not guilty," Winston said. "Your Honor, please, I would like a law—"

"Ho—heh-heh, stop right there son. Ah, ah still cunt hear ya, ah cunt, ah cunt, you cunt!" The judge turned to his court officer, smiling like a mischievous twelve-year-old. "Officer, officer, did you hear what Allah's little fuckbuddy said just now, ah am having trouble hearing him?"

"Why, yes, Your Honor, I did hear what he said," answered the court officer.

"And, pray tell, Homeland Security Court Officer of God's United States, what did he say?"

"He said guilty as charged, Your Honor, to both charges."

The judge slammed his gavel down.

"Will the federal prosecutor enter the plea of guilty as charged to the felony crime of subversive behavior in the first degree and the felony crime of marijuana possession?"

The small man in the suit entered information into a palmtop computer. "So entered, Your Honor." He had not said a word until now. For the first time, Winston realized that the man he had hoped was his lawyer was the federal prosecutor.

"And what do the People request in way of a sentence, and I would think that the People would want to make sure that this junkie Subversive does not infect others with his ideological cancer, Steve, am I right?"

"Your Honor, the People request ultimate rehabilitation at a Homeland Security special prison," the prosecutor replied.

"Winston Smith, this court sentences you to five years of ultimate rehabilitation in a Homeland Security special prison, and may Jesus Christ our Lord and Savior have mercy on your heathen, drug-addicted soul!" The judge loudly banged his gavel, and the prison guards began zipping the dark hood back over Winston's shoulders.

"WAIT!" Winston shrieked at the top of his lungs before they could finish closing the zipper over his head. "Your Honor, please, I said NOT Guilty, I never said guilt—"

"Guards, you will restrain this convict, he is ranting and menacing this court and I will not stand for it!" The judge's face was inflamed red, and he hammered the gavel against the table incessantly.

As the zipper was yanked shut, an electric shock pierced Winston's back, spreading through his body in a hot flash as he lost consciousness.

Eleven

By the time the prison guards unzipped his incarceration suit, Winston had been alert for a few hours. Although he could not recall the journey that brought him to the prison, he was aware that he, in his body bag, had been hooked onto a cart, then wheeled from a van through a long hallway. Someone had rehung the bag and left him for what seemed like a long time.

The light blinded his eyes as his hood was removed. Two burly guards in Homeland Security uniforms, their tall black leather boots glistening, peeled the incarceration suit from his body.

Winston slowly turned his head. He was in a tiny, sparkling steel prison cell. One of the guards, with a long scar under his chin, quickly fastened a thin metallic collar around his neck. Then both guards moved toward the door.

"Wait," Winston stammered, "What—what am I supposed to do now? Can I make a call? I need to make a call."

A searing pain ripped across his back. The guard with the scar was pressing a small wireless device that controlled the pain delivery through the collar. "I'll say this once, shithead. Speak when you're spoken to."

The other guard chimed in, with a deep, menacing voice. "They don't pay us enough to have to listen to youse whining cocksuckers."

"Hey Joe, we got time to play with commie queerbait a little more?" the guard with the scar asked, as he notched up the pain level. "Maybe I could grab us a broomstick from the janitor room."

Winston fell to his knees as the pain exploded from his spine. "Ahhh . . . please!" he begged.

"I warned you to shut the fuck up!" The guard turned the pain level even higher as Winston cringed on the floor.

The second guard unlocked the cell door and headed to the hallway. "C'mon Nick, we gotta report in five minutes."

"You one lucky raghead motherfucker," Nick said, leaving the cell.

Winston stretched out on the hard cold floor, waiting for the pain to dissipate. He slowly made his way to the solitary small cot, and lay across it, stretching his body out for the first time in days.

He looked around. The cell had no window, just the cot, and an open toilet. He was surprised to find himself in the same clothes he had been wearing when he arrived at the airport. The only thing missing was his wallet. His body still aching, he drifted into a deep sleep.

Winston woke to the sound of a steady tapping nearby. The upbeat tune sounded familiar. He listened for a while with his eyes closed, trying to place it. He hoped that when he opened his eyes he would be at home, that this was all a nightmare. A man's voice started singing the familiar melody. He opened his eyes, and his heart sank at the sight of the dismal cell. The singer seemed to be in the cell next to his.

"Oh should the sun, refuse to shine, oh should that sun refuse to shine . . . You know I want to be in that number, oh should the sun refuse to shine . . . Oh when the saints, come marching in, oh when the saints come marching in . . ."

The singer continued with another verse. Then he moved to the bars of his cell, and spoke in a hushed, familiar tone. "Welcome to hell, brother."

Winston moved to the bars of his cell so he could hear better. "Where are we?"

"Doesn't matter, brother. In five days we'll both be dead."

"The judge sentenced me to five years, not execution," Winston protested. "But there was a strange . . . a strange . . ."

"Finality about it. You're not imagining things. I was given just two years for subversive protest. But it was two years of what they call 'ultimate rehabilitation.' So here in Homeland Security 'special' prison, what's so special is that the number of years is meaningless, it's just for their official court records. It's really the same for everyone. On the fifth day after you arrive," the man paused and his voice quivered, "they let a gang of sadistic thugs beat you to death."

"You are shittin' me," Winston replied, annoyed. "Look, I know this place is bugged, and I don't know what your racket is. But I've had a pretty fucked up week."

"Five solitary holding cells," the man continued, ominously. "Yesterday I was in your cell. Today they moved me here to make room for you. One cell closer to what they call the 'playpen.' That's the open dormitory they release you to, filled with a dozen of the most sadistic, violent killers and rapists in the entire federal prison system. They're the ones who kill you." His voice grew weak with fright. "Any way they choose."

"Fuck you!" Winston cursed, and backed up to his cot.

"I wish I was joking. Before you got here they carried out today's victim. He hung himself before they could transfer him. That's what most guys do. The prison plans it that way. It's why they leave you with your belt and shoelaces."

Winston noticed that he indeed still had his belt and laces on. He moved closer to the cell bars.

"You either kill yourself, or the other convicts torture and kill you. In the peace movement, we call this the 'General Bashcrost Special.'"

Winston was surprised to hear that there still was a peace movement. He knew that his mother had called herself a peace activist, but she had fled to Costa Rica in 2009, with hundreds of thousands of other peaceniks, right before the revised Constitution took effect.

"Peace movement?" Winston asked. "I thought that went out—"

"With opposition parties and free speech? Nope, some of us stayed, still working, through churches and community groups in the ghettos. What's your name, brother?"

"Name's Winston. Do you really go around calling everyone brother?"

"Yup. My name's Brian O'Neil, from the people's ghetto of Bed-Stuy, Brooklyn. And we're all brothers in the eyes of Christ, even our torturers. It's about forgiveness, the greatest challenge of all."

"I take it you're some sort of religious activist?"

"Uh-huh. Though not in the mold of General Bashcrost. I'm a Catholic Worker, Winston. Ever heard of us?"

"I remember something about that group from years ago. Some Lower East Side Saint, or something?"

"Dorothy Day, our group's founder. Try to emulate Jesus in your own life, through deeds, not words. Simple as that. To me, that means that Jesus would have been out there last week, just like I was, on Good Friday, pouring blood on the ground outside of the Intrepid aircraft carrier museum, to protest our society's celebration of killing and militarism."

Winston could not believe Brian's stupidity. "You must have known you would be arrested?"

"I knew there was a chance of it, a good chance of it."

"Were you alone?"

"Uh-huh, although there were plenty of tourists watching. Even more than when I got arrested there ten years ago, to commemorate my thirtieth birthday. Difference this time was, for my fortieth birthday, it was an individual instead of a group action, and there was no media. And the cops were rougher, a lot rougher. Worst of all, the sentence—I . . . I still can't believe they sentenced me to this place."

"The world's changed a lot in the last ten years," Winston said, intent on ensuring that whoever might be listening to the bugged cellblock would know he was still a Patriotic Citizen. He wasn't going to bad-mouth his government, no matter how he was baited. "The world's a lot more dangerous than it was ten years ago. We have the terrorists to thank for that!"

"It sure is more dangerous," Brian said. "But that wouldn't have made a difference to Jesus."

"You're not Jesus."

"Never said I was. Hope against fear, brother, hope against fear."

At the far end of the hall, they could hear a gate opening. Winston stepped back and sat on his cot, listening. Brian, he noticed, at least had the sense to keep his mouth shut when the guards were around.

Nick and Joe, the guards that had left him in the cell earlier, entered the cellblock with two other guards. They all carried long electronic shock prods. Nick, the guard with the scar, passed Winston's cell. He pulled a small shrink-wrapped box from a bag, dropped it to the floor, and kicked it under the bars to where Winston sat on his cot.

"Wuff-wuff," Nick barked. "Mealtime."

Winston was starving. He bent over and eagerly started peeling the plastic off the box. It read, "Homeland Protective Services Corporation, D-Ration."

"Psst, hey queerbait," Nick stuck his face between the bars, nodded in the direction of the far end of the hall, and winked.

The scar across his neck seemed to throb with delight. "Listen up real good to the show!" Nick pulled the small pain collar controller from his pocket and pressed a button. "BEEP!" he squeaked.

The pain shot instantly from Winston's steel collar down through his back. He dropped the meal box and fell to the floor, convulsing in pain.

Nick burst into laughter. "Hey Joe," the guard said to the other. "I told you he could swim." They moved on to the next cell.

"Wuff-wuff," Winston heard the guard say to Brian, kicking a box of food across the floor. "BEEP!"

"Aaaiieeggh!" Brian screamed.

The pain across Winston's body diminished, and his hunger grew. He ripped open the box as he heard Nick repeat the routine at the two other solitary cells further down the hall, followed by screams of pain.

In the D-ration box were three pieces of white bread that felt like plastic, a half liter plastic container of water, and a quarter pound slab of pink substance labeled, "Made with Real Meat."

Winston shoved the food in his mouth, barely slowing down to chew. He was finished in less than a minute, then slowly drank the water. Wondering what the guards were doing down the hall, he stood closer to the bars, and listened.

He heard the guards unlock a cell door, then a scuffle.

"You can't make me go—ahhhh!" A prisoner seemed to be resisting being dragged out by the guards, until the familiar sound of agony from the pain collar left him screaming.

For a moment there was silence, then a body being dragged in the direction opposite Winston in the cell block.

Soon a new sound rose, not a word, but a low-pitched, guttural chant, from a dozen throats, that grew louder and louder, which was joined by the thunderous stomping of boots. "Huuah . . . huuah . . . huuah . . . huuah . . ."

The chant went on for five minutes, "Huuah . . . huuah . . .

huuah . . . huuah . . ." It was broken by a prison guard's voice, amplified by a speaker.

"Step back from the gate, you know the drill. That's right, don't make us use the riot sticks. There's enough B-rations in the cart for you each to have five, so don't fight over them. We've got a new friend for you to meet."

Winston heard a large door swing open with a creak.

"Count to fifty, boys," the amplified guard's voice said. "Count to fifty."

The gate clanged shut. There was an eerie calm as the guards sauntered back up the hall. Winston quickly moved to the wall away from his cell's doors. Nick pressed his scarred face through the bars again. "Listen good, you God-hating cocksucker. Your day is coming. We gotta go patrol the perimeter now. BEEP!"

The pain erupted again from Winston's collar.

The guards laughed as they headed out of the hallway. "Patrol the perimeter," one of them repeated. "Nick, you crack me up."

The gate to the cellblock slammed shut with a deafening clang.

Then it began. The first sound Winston heard was a swift rush of movement, then, a cacophony of taunts, followed by the thuds of blows. "You're mine, pretty boy, all mine, all mine, mine!" a husky, angry voice yelled. "My turn!" another voice interrupted, followed by a yelp of pain, then a scream, an agonizing scream.

The screams were interrupted only by the powerful thuds of objects being smashed against bones.

"Aiiiiiiiiii . . . pleassssssse . . ." the condemned man screamed.

"No cutting yet, hold off on the shank or I'll fuck you up," a voice threatened.

"He's mine, gimme him back, I said he's mine," the other husky voice repeated.

There was the sound of fighting. The victim's cries grew more wretched, but weaker, ever weaker, as the torture continued. The screams became whimpers, and then stopped.

"Me next," a new voice asserted, quickly followed by, "My turn."

Winston withdrew to his cot and wrapped the one blanket around his head, trying to muffle the noise. He was too depressed to ask Brian more questions. From the moment he heard the tortured cries of the condemned man, Winston understood that Brian's bleak characterization had been true.

He curled up in his bed, grateful for the warmth of the small blanket, trying desperately to shut out the world around him. But the convicts only got louder, asserting their claims, boasting of sexual acts.

Howls of fighting and carousing persisted through the night from what Brian had called the "playpen." Winston tried to close his mind to the grotesque sounds that haunted him. But with each eruption of whoops and screams of cruel ecstasy, gruesome pictures filled his head. Four more days, he thought, four more days and it's my turn.

It was only at dawn, hours after the noise ceased, that Winston fell into a tormented sleep.

TWELVE

Winston did not want to wake up. Only the fear of the guards jolting his pain collar brought him to his feet. That, and an urgent need to piss.

Within moments, he heard Brian whistling a tune, and walked to the edge of his cell. "Pssst," Winston hissed, attracting his neighbor's attention. "I'm starving. Do we get fed again, or is starving to death part of the package?"

"Back in the day," Brian explained, "people spoke of an inmate's three square meals. That was before the reform they called privatization. These days, Homeland Protective Agencies, a subsidiary of Hullibarton, owns the prison and supplies the meals."

"Vice President Croney's company owns them?"

"Yeah, lucky guy, that Croney, able to draw two salaries since they put him back on top there. Hullibarton gets a flat per-day fee per prisoner, for one meal or three. I'd love to know what they charge Uncle Sam for our D-rations."

"Free enterprise built this country," Winston countered, on behalf of the surveillance cameras.

"Brother, maybe they did make a mistake putting you in here."

"Fucken right they did. If I could only get a call out—"

The cell block hall door opened. Winston shut up and backed into his cot.

"Moving time in five minutes!" Nick yelled down the hall, as he entered the cell block with three other prison guards, one driving a cart. Nick poked his face through Winston's cell bars, waving his finger menacingly over his pain controller. "Hope you liked yesterday's concert, queerbait," Nick taunted. "Bet you'd love to see our video surveillance. But hold onto your boner—your turn comes soon. Now grab your dress and lipstick and get ready to move closer to your ultimate rehabilitation. Oh, yeah, I almost forgot—BEEP!" Nick screeched, then pressed down the pain controller, throwing Winston again to the ground in convulsions of pain.

Laughing, Nick joined the others as they headed toward the far end of the cell block. "Hey Nick, lookie what we got here," another guard shouted.

"A double pick-up," Nick yelled back, delighted. "Saves us an afternoon release. What'd you doodie do to yourself, you bad boy . . ."

Brian's voice whispered from the adjoining cell. "Sounds like a suicide. Poor guy probably did it during the night."

"Listening to the torture, knowing you're next," Winston closed his eyes. "God, this can't really be happening."

"Dorothy Day used to say that the love of God is a harsh and dangerous love," Brian said. "I pray that I can find my way there."

Winston fingered his shoes. "I'm glad they leave you with your laces," he said gloomily.

"They send your family notice that you've killed yourself. Or, if their goons kill you, they say you had an accident. Case closed.

Worst part for me is that I can't kill myself." Brian sounded conflicted. "It's against everything I believe in."

An amplified guard's voice boomed orders to the convicts in the large pen at the far end of the cellblock. "Bring the body to the door of the pen and move to the rear. You know the drill."

"Leave some towels to clean up this fucken mess, Turner," a husky voice countered. "And you fucken better have some A-rations in your cart today."

"I said back to the wall or you'll be swimming on that stinking floor for an hour," the guard's amplified voice warned. "That means you, Jones. Now get the fuck back! We've got two A-ration cartons and two cartons of cigarettes."

The door of the large pen clanged shut, then two cell doors near it were opened. "Cut down the body you find hanging in your new cell, pissworm," the guard on the amplifier yelled to the inmate two cells away from Winston's. "Load him in the cart, then get back in his cell. Tomorrow will be your big day."

The men in the holding pen erupted into brutal taunts and chants of "huua-aahhh." Then a convict's voice yelled, "Fuck tomorrow. Give us a new fish today!" Other men shouted their agreement.

A guard opened Winston's cell. "Move, queerbait, now." Winston walked into the dark, concrete hallway, just as Brian was being herded into the vacated cell adjoining his.

Brian glanced at Winston over his shoulder, and pressed his hand to his heart, a simple gesture that somehow seemed courageous and defiant. He was larger than Winston had imagined, a burly, wild-haired man with a long unkempt beard, dressed in faded jeans and an old tee shirt.

Nick stood next to the electric cart as he waited in the hall for Winston. The cart's open back held two corpses, covered with an old sheet.

"Hey, queerbait, here's your gourmet dinner," Nick said, tossing Winston his daily box of D-rations. "And lookee here . . . someone had an accident."

Nick peeled the sheet back over the corpses. Alongside the lifeless body of the hanged inmate lay the naked, mutilated remains of the man who had been murdered the previous night. Small pools of blood formed on the rubber sheet beneath him. Winston could not turn away from the disgusting sight. The torture had been so brutal that he could not even distinguish between parts of the dead man's body.

Winston cupped his hands around his mouth to catch a sudden surge of vomit.

"Take that inside, buttboy," Nick grabbed Winston and threw him hard across the hallway, toward what had been Brian's cell. "I hears you was hot shit in the big city, a big swinging dick before you betrayed our country. Now you queerbait for the bad boys to play with, and you gonna end up just like this sorry fuck. Now get the fuck in there," Nick commanded, kicking Winston savagely in his side, sending him sprawling into the cell. Nick slammed the cell door shut, and spit a wad of phlem into Winston's face.

"That's for all the red-blooded Americans that're dying 'cause of scum like you," he yelled. "Three more days and it's your turn. Your new friends'll make you a real man!"

Although terribly hungry, Winston decided against eating his rations while he felt sick. He rinsed his mouth with some water, and then started searching his tiny cell for something that he might sharpen to use as a weapon to fight off the sadistic convicts when he was released into the "playpen."

He realized the stupidity of the effort and stopped. The anticipation was tearing him apart. He wished he had a book, a TV, anything to take his mind off the image of the mangled corpse, the dying man's tortured screams, the sounds of the sadists just a hundred feet down the hall from him.

Winston squatted down and yanked the laces from his shoe. "I don't have to play this fucken game," he murmured aloud. Standing on his cot, he tied the laces together, attached one to a shoe, and tried tossing it over an exposed sprinkler pipe that hung conveniently from the ceiling. He missed the pipe, cursed out loud, and tried again.

Brian called out, in a caring voice, from the nearby cell. "What're you up to, brother?"

"None of your fucken business, brother," Winston snarled back.

"You said you'd be out of here if you could make a call," Brian offered. "Isn't it too soon to give up hope?"

Winston missed the pipe again. He got off the cot and stomped to his cell's bars. "Oh, you think our good pal Nick is gonna get me a phone?"

"All I'm saying," Brian coolly replied, "is that whoever you were going to call might be on his way as we speak. Wouldn't it be a shame if you hung yourself right before the cavalry arrived?"

"Maybe . . . maybe you got a point. I can always do it later, before they send me in to be killed. But maybe you're just trying to talk me out of it because you're too scared to do it yourself?"

"It's not fear of the action, Winston, it's fear of the spiritual reaction. How can I throw away the gift that is this life?"

"Wake up and smell the blood, doofus! I'm not feeling much like God's gift 'round here." But he decided to wait a while.

The next two days passed in painful monotony. At noon, Winston and the other inmates were moved one cell closer to the open dormitory, and then a new inmate was moved into the fifth solitary cell. The guards tortured each day's newcomer with the pain collar until he "swam," then laughed and bragged about it in the hallway. The killers in the dormitory at the end of the cell-block erupted into murderous chants a few times a day, with syn-chronized stomping, obscene threats, and blood-curdling, animal-like howls. On Winton's third day, the inmate on deck for release into the dormitory hung himself, again robbing the sadists of an opportunity to torture him to death.

The repulsive D-ration meals of plastic white bread and pink meat substance came once a day, at noon, when the cell move happened. Winston spent the time perpetually hungry with nothing to do except wait for the inevitable to happen on his fifth day. He talked to Brian through the bars, and prayed that help would somehow arrive in time.

"I have to believe that the people I work with don't know what happened to me," he confided to Brian, on his fourth day, right after the guards had moved them into their new solitary cells, closer to their deaths. "My girlfriend will tell them. Then they'll find some bug in the system that caught me, and pull strings to fix it. If I could only get to a phone . . ."

"I'm afraid the system is the bug," Brian replied angrily, terrified of what would happen later in the day. "The bug is the people's acquiescence to a murderous, totalitarian state."

"I'm sure these halls are wired," Winston warned.

"What are they gonna do to me?" Brian challenged. "They can only kill a man once, and the torture I'm likely to endure three hours from now is about the most horrible death I can imagine. Hey, General Bashcrost," he yelled. "Kiss my poor white Christian ass! 'Cause there's a very special place in hell for hypocrites like you!"

"Tone it down," Winston advised. "We don't need to spend our last hours whimpering on the floor in pain from these fucken collars."

"Fuck 'em!" Brain cursed. "Hope against fear!" he yelled, at the top of his lungs. "Hope against fear!"

"What did you mean death by torture?" Winston asked, in a confidential whisper, hoping that Brian would quiet down. "You've got laces and a belt, don't you?"

"Sure do," Brian replied, now quieter. "But I can't bring myself to use it. At four o'clock, my life will be in the hands of God."

"You heard what happened a few days ago—what kept happening all night long!" Winston said, more urgently. "They'll tear you to pieces—you heard it with your own ears."

"Did you know they've got crematoriums attached to every one of the hundred-plus Homeland Security special prisons?" Brian explained. "Your ashes get sent home in a cheap plastic box, with a short Homeland Security form letter saying that you had an accident, when they murder you, or that you committed suicide, when you kill yourself. My wife Mariah has been in the Resistance for six years now, since we moved into the ghetto. She'll know the difference when she gets that letter, and so will our daughter, when she gets older. It's ashes either way, eventually it's all ashes, in here or not. Jesus knew that. He walked to his own death, bearing love and forgiveness in his heart. Mariah will understand that. She'll read it was an 'accident,' then one day tell our daughter Tara that I did not give up my faith in God's grace, that no matter what, I did not give up my faith."

"Spare yourself the pain of—"

"Life is pain," Brian interrupted. "Pain and hope. But why surrender hope? Maybe I can speak with the other convicts—tell them what I'm in here for. Maybe there will be a few among them who still have Jesus in their hearts, a few who will protect me from the others."

Winston shook his head sadly. "Brother, I don't think they would have been chosen to staff that playpen if Jesus were anywhere near their hearts."

"You're probably right," Brian sounded resigned and frightened. "All I can do is try my best to enter that lion's den with love in my heart for all men, even my attackers, even . . . even the misguided hypocrites who sent me here."

Brian's voice grew stronger, more resolute. "Hope against fear, brother, hope against fear!"

What else can I say, Winston thought, as he backed up to his cot? He lay there, depressed, listening to the murmurs of Brian's prayers.

At four o'clock, the four-guard squad passed slowly by Winston's cell. Winston had heard Nick screech "BEEP" as he passed each of the other three cells. He backed himself as far from the hall as possible, hoping the distance would lessen the inevitable jolt to his pain collar. "BEEP!" Nick yelled, throwing Winston to the floor with convulsions stabbing down his back, into his legs, neck and head.

From the floor, Winston listened as Brian's cell door was unlocked.

"I'd like to confess," Brian asked, stepping into the hallway. "May I see a priest?"

"A priest?" Nick acted surprised, while the other guards laughed at his performance. "Why on earth would you need a priest? Your new friends are the salt of the earth."

Brian spoke his confessions quickly, but the words were drowned out by the stomping from the dormitory cell, and the brutal chant, "Huuuah! Huuu-ahh! Huu-ah!"

A guard made his voice heard through large speakers. "Stand against the back wall, gentlemen, you know the drill, stand back and count to fifty."

A gate was unlocked. Winston pictured Brian stepping forward. The gate was slammed shut. Winston lay on his cot, and pressed the blanket to his ears to muffle the sound.

"Brothers," he heard Brian say, loudly, while the guards headed out of the cellblock. "You don't have to do this. Jesus showed us that it is never too late for compassion, for love, for redemp—ahhhhhhhhggghhhhhh!"

The assault began. Winston buried his head deeper into the mattress, but the noise was everywhere. Taunts, blows, arguments between the sadistic killers over whose turn it was, screams of pain, shrieks of agony, cries of cruel ecstasy. Then, moans of agony, which grew weaker and weaker, until Winston could hear only the jubilant murderers playing with their victim's corpse.

The arguments, cries and obscene claims continued through the night. Winston lay on his bed, trembling. The fear consumed him. He was struck blind by it, pressing his face against the mattress. Every thought, every image he tried to conjure up to interrupt the movie of what was happening in the dormitory next to him disappeared the instant it surfaced. He held the blanket so tightly around his head that he wondered if it would smother him. He hoped that it would.

Somehow, in the middle of the night, Winston fell asleep, even before the sounds subsided, right before dawn. His dreams, even his nightmares, were a welcome relief.

He awoke to the sound of Nick screeching "BEEP," and the yelps of pain of the inmates up the hall. It was nearly noon, he thought, of his last day on earth. He hurried to the open toilet before the guards reached him. It felt good to urinate, to still be alive. I'm not ready to die, he told himself.

A prison guard swung open his cell. "You're still here, shithead," Nick announced. "Get moving. This is your big day!"

Winston stepped out and rushed into the open cell next door before one of the guards could kick him. Nick and Joe followed him in, while the other two guards waited in the hall with their cart.

"Here's a razor, in case you want to pretty yourself up for the boys," Nick said, tossing it on the cot, with a slightly larger shrink-wrapped food box. "Here—you get a C-ration today, 'cause we're such nice guys."

"Help me," Winston pleaded, moving closer to his jailer. "I need to make just one call. I can pay you. Name the price. I can transfer money anywhere you want. I . . . I've got enough to take good care of you, you and the other guards and even the warden."

"Oh, and what then, asswipe?", Nick replied, skeptical. The scar across his neck throbbed with anger. "You get outta here, Homeland Security has a record of every step of your journey, then their boot comes down on me and the warden and Joe here, and before we know, it, we're trading places. I don't think so, queerbait."

"But I'm here by mistake—"

"You had your chance with the judge. That's the American way. Meanwhile, what're you worried about? You got eighty virgins waiting to get you off in heaven. Isn't that what you Muslim freaks believe?"

Nick and Joe laughed mercilessly.

"I was raised a Christian," Winston replied, "not a Mus—"

"I hopes he don't gotta be a virgin to get to Allah's pearly gates," Joe interrupted. "After his coming-out party with the boys at four, he ain't gonna be any kind of a virgin."

"What happens at four?" Winston asked, trying to keep the conversation going.

"What happens," Nick replied, winking at Joe. "Nothing happens, we just transfer you into a regular cell, no more need for solitary and segregation. You get to mix it up with the general population."

"But they—they'll kill me!"

"Why would they do that, buttboy? Why you think like that? Hey Joe, you hear this kind of talking?"

"Sad day in the country when a man don't feel safe in a federal prison run by a reputable concern like Hullibarton," Joe replied, with a wide smile. "But I bet my old pal Bobby, who's fighting in Pakistan right this moment, ain't feeling too safe now, neither. Meanwhile, we gotta baby-sit these whining faggots that're helping the enemy undermine us, sucking down good rations from Uncle Sam's tit!"

"He probably thinks we're gonna keep him five years in solitary and segregation."

"Maybe he'd like room service, HBO and waterbeds, too?" Joe added.

Nick laughed heartily at Joe's joke. "Hey, hey cocksucker—you want a mint for your pillow when we drop you in the playpen at four?"

Joe laughed meanly. "You gonna be a big hit in your new community, a handsome strapping queerboy like you! Maybe you'll be so popular they'll let youse live till the next morning!"

"No one's that popular, Joe," Nick said, looking Winston over. "Two hundred bucks says he's gone in under thirty minutes."

"I'm not taking that fucken bet. Make it under twenty minutes and three-to-one odds."

"Twenty minutes and two-to-one on two hundred."

"Done. I win, you pays me four hundred. You're on," Joe agreed.

The guards shook on their bet and headed for the cell door.

"Wait," Winston cried. "I'm not asking you to arrange my release. Just bring me a phone for twenty minutes. I'll pay you fifty thousand dollars to use a phone. I can make some calls and have this straightened out in twenty minutes. My being here is a terrible mistake, and if—"

"Our government don't make mistakes. Later, big man . . . BEEP!" Nick screeched, as he suddenly tapped the pain controller, leaving Winston yelping in pain.

The men joined the other guards in the hall, slamming and locking Winston's cell door behind them.

"Yo, listen up gentlemen," Nick yelled, in the direction of the dormitory cell. "We got a cute one for you, four o'clock today! Right now, we need you to bring the body to the door, then stand against the far wall . . ."

Winston shut himself in the darkness of his blanket and forced himself not to look at the cart that the guards drove past his cell.

A horrible chant arose from the large "playpen" cell nearby. "You! You! You! You!" A dozen voices chanted in unison. The nearby killers stomped their boots. The noise was deafening.

Winston looked at the ceiling of his cell. The sturdily-fastened sprinkler pipe attached to the ceiling had scuffmarks from countless suicides past. He thought of the Homeland Security inmates who preceded him, and those in hundreds of prisons just like this one. What had they done, he wondered?

Were any of them real terrorists, or just citizens, like him, who wound up on the wrong side of the new Patriot Act?

Winston stood on the cot, and fastened his belt to the pipe. The chants from the next cell had been replaced with an endless tirade of brutal threats, unnerving him. The convicts seemed to compete for who could concoct the most vulgar threat, laced with recollections of past acts.

Winston's hands trembled, and it took him a while to tie his laces together. He fastened them with a slipknot to the hanging belt. He tested the noose with his wrist. It worked.

Winston looked at his watch. It was just twelve-thirty and he was ready. He would give himself to three o'clock, and then end his life. That would give him time to slit his wrists with the razor if a lace broke, or something else went wrong.

Sitting on the bed, Winston closed his eyes and tried to shut out the loud taunts. There was time, he thought, to reflect on his life, to meditate, to pray. But all that came to him was anger toward a system that would murder him for no good reason, and anger at himself for spending his entire adult life defending and promoting this system. What a sucker I've been, he thought. Tears streamed down his cheeks, and he buried his head in his hands, sobbing.

Suddenly, he heard Nick's harsh voice just yards from his door. The taunts from the nearby dormitory had been so loud that he had not heard the cellblock door open.

Winston wiped his face dry and jumped up. In their hatefulness and spite, he realized, the guards were coming early, to rob him of the option of taking his own life.

He stuck his head in the makeshift noose and jumped off the bed.

"Aaaagggggggggggggghhhh," he groaned, focusing his mind on not letting his hands move toward the noose. First he lost his breath. Then darkness began to envelope him. Soon it would be over, he thought, and a calm feeling of acceptance warmed the darkness.

THIRTEEN

The next thing he knew, Winston was lying across the floor, a sliced shoelace around his neck. Two steel-toed black boots were kicking him in the back.

"Get the fuck up, maggot," Nick ordered. Winston stood painfully, slowly regaining his senses.

Nick gestured to the open cell door while dangling the pain controller menacingly. "Come with us."

"You gots a visitor," the other guard added. "He wants to talk wit' you."

Winston stumbled out of the cell into the hallway. "Where the fuck you taking him!" an aggrieved voice from the neighboring dormitory cell demanded, amidst a growing chorus of taunts.

"For a little walk. He'll be back at four," Nick said.

Winston marched silently between the two guards. They led him through three secure gates, into a large elevator, then through a long, cement hall until they arrived at a small business office, with a meeting table and fully-equipped work desk.

"Sit down," Nick gestured to an interrogation chair next to the meeting table. It had wheels and restraint straps for wrists, ankles and neck. Winston sat unsteadily as Nick secured the straps.

Were they looking for confessions, Winston wondered? Would they torture him for his last hours of life, seeking information on imagined accomplices?

The guards backed away to the door and spoke with someone there. The voice was familiar. The person entered and closed the door behind him, but the restraint stopped Winston from turning to look. A second later, the enormous body of his boss, Neil Swan, plopped down in the chair facing him.

"Hello, Prisoner Smith," Swan said, shaking his pudgy head disapprovingly. "Look at the mess you've gotten yourself into."

"I . . . I'm so sorry . . ."

"You ask for approval for *1984*," Swan continued, as though reading an indictment. "I say no. I order you to burn the scripts. I authorize a three-week vacation, recommend Las Vegas. But it's not my role to baby-sit you. So after the fact—without a fucken word—without even giving the man who built your entire fucken career single-handedly the courtesy of being informed, you run off like some terrorist and sell the fucken script to the BBC! And, oh yes, by the way, I am told—again not from you—I am told that the BBC's film is being set in modern day America and that Winston Smith—the very Winston Smith I have mentored for more than ten fucken years—Winston Smith is ghost-writing the changes. It's like I'm walking around the ministry with a sign on my back that says, 'Fuck Me—I'm Easy.'" Swan watched Winston carefully.

"I'm . . . I'm so sorry. Neil," Winston thought of what would happen if he didn't get out of prison that day and tears swelled in his eyes.

"Spare me the theatrics, Prisoner Smith. I'm sure you're very sorry that you got caught. But we have a history. You were a Party member once upon a time. Loyalty may mean nothing to you, but it means something to us. So I'm here to see if you're willing to do what it takes to get you transferred to another prison."

"Please, Neil, please," Winston begged. "I'm so sorry. I don't want to die here. I'll do anything."

"It won't be cheap, Prisoner Smith. You've messed things up in a big way. It's very rare that anyone gets transferred out of a Homeland Security special prison."

"Just name it. Any price, anything."

Swan unfolded a piece of paper with numbers scrawled on it and took out a pen. "You'll need to reimburse the government for your transport, trial and care. That's four hundred thousand dollars, plus a fifty-percent Party surcharge. That's six hundred thousand dollars."

"Six hundred thousand dollars?" Winston gulped.

Swan looked at him sternly and cocked an eyebrow.

"Of course," Winston nodded approvingly. "Six hundred thousand dollars. I can take care of it."

"I know you can," Swan continued. "I know what we pay you and I've seen your bank balance. The Party has been good to you."

"Of course it has, Neil. And I'll make it up to them—to you."

Swan looked skeptical. "That part's coming. First, the money. You've also got my travel expenses, taking time off and having to charter a copter to come out here to Buttfuck, Georgia. That's another one hundred fifty thousand dollars, which goes to my Cayman Islands account. I'll give you the wire transfer numbers when the warden logs you into the computer."

"As good as done," Winston agreed.

"Then there's the matter of . . . gratuities. This doesn't happen often. Your sentencing judge gets one hundred twenty thousand dollars for transfer consideration. The warden expects one hundred thousand. The guards less."

Winston swallowed hard and nodded. "Give me access to a secure line and I'll make the transfers right now."

"I'm sure you will, boy, I'm sure you will. But that's only part of the deal."

Winston waited. He had already promised nearly two-thirds of his life savings. "What else, Mr. Swan?"

"The only way I can get you out of here is if you erase what you've done."

"How do I do that?" Winston asked.

"You've got to stop the BBC from making this movie. That's the only way that General Bashcrost and Minister of Truth Limetoff will commute your sentence. You're in deep shit right now, and that's the one thing that will convince them that you've dug your way out of it. Kill the project, and they can forget about you. Then we could see about getting you paroled early, perhaps even to your old job."

"There's nothing I would love more, Neil. I'll do . . . I'll do whatever it takes. Do you want to send me back to England?"

Swan laughed. "That's a good one. I'm glad to see you haven't lost your sense of humor. No, you're not leaving the country for an amnesty-granting, disloyal ex-ally, probably not ever again. Here's the deal: make the payments now, agree to call the BBC later tonight, and you can be transferred immediately to a lower security prison labor camp. We could keep a close eye on you there, until this project is officially killed by the BBC. And believe me, we'll know whether that happens or not."

Winston's mind raced ahead to the call he needed to make, to how he would phrase his dilemma. Paul would understand. It was a matter of life and death. "It . . . it may take a little time."

"Then we have an understanding," Swan concluded, looking at his watch. "I'll call the warden in and you can make the wire transfers."

"Fine, great. Listen, Neil, do you realize that if you had arrived just a quarter hour later, I would have been dead? I had already hung myself back there."

"Hung yourself," Swan asked, playing dumb. "Why would you do an insane thing like that?"

"Why?" Winston's eyes bulged and he realized his hand was

trembling. "Because in less than three hours I would have been released into a locked cell full of killers and rapists, who would have torn me apart just like they did to two other inmates before me."

Swan stared at him, dead serious. "Am I supposed to find this amusing?"

"It's the truth, Neil! I heard it happen twice. I saw the goddamned corpses!"

"Ahhhhhhhh, the truth" Swan nodded slowly. "The truth, to you, perhaps. To me, it sounds like prison suicides are common, and sometimes, accidents do happen." Swan smiled cruelly. "Perhaps you hallucinated that an accident was something it wasn't. Perhaps you need to stay here, rest some more, get a psychiatric evaluation. Shall I arrange one with the prison doctor, and we can forget this whole . . . transfer business?"

"No! No, please, Neil, please. Forget . . . forget my overactive imagination." Winston realized that Swan knew just what he was doing. He forced a grin. "Please . . . just tell me what I need to do to get transferred out of here. Anything . . ."

"You'll be going to a privatized work camp for drug violators and light Subversives," Swan said. He nodded knowingly toward the door. "You can see what happens to the serious Subversives. Don't worry. No violent terrorists where you'll be going, just lost souls being taught a hard lesson about our government's commitment to the War on Drugs and the War on Terrorist Speech. You'll have a bed, a full time agricultural job—whatever that means—plus three square meals. I think that about four hundred dollars a day, plus the Party surcharge of fifty percent, will get you decent A-Class accommodations and rations. From what I hear of the food," Swan offered a friendly smile, "spending the money would be highly advisable."

"Of course," Winston agreed. The place sounded like paradise.

"You're lucky, Prisoner Smith," Swan said solemnly, "to get a second chance, after what you've done."

"What I . . . ?" Winston caught his words mid-sentence and told himself to shut up.

Swan's face hardened. The fat under his chin trembled slightly as he gritted his teeth and watched Winston closely. "What's that you were saying?"

"What I've . . . what I've been meaning to do since the moment you got here is thank you, Neil," Winston continued. "On a personal level, what I . . . can't recall is anyone sticking their neck out for me the way you have, coming all the way out here, despite my . . . lapse of judgment and disloyal behavior."

Tears of appreciation rolled down Winston's cheeks. He reached his arms out and put them around Swan's massive bulk. "You're like a father to me, Neil, ever since my father was murdered by those terrorist bastards."

"Pull yourself together, son." Swan said, sitting back and looking at his watch. "It's time to put your money where your mouth is."

With great effort, Swan lifted his massive body out of the chair, walked to the door, and opened it. "Officer," he said politely to one of the guards who had brought Winston in. "Could you please ask the warden to join us?"

Nick and Joe returned with a tall, skinny man about Winston's age in a narrow suit and a black leather bolo tie. They stood as Neil Swan sat back down.

"Warden Moore, this extremely contrite young prisoner is begging Homeland Security for a second chance at rehabilitation elsewhere, by serving out his term in an agricultural labor camp."

"Have you reached an understanding with the prisoner regarding the Minister of Truth's concerns?" the warden asked, deferentially.

"Yes," Swan nodded. "With the monitoring provisions we discussed earlier."

"Very well then," the warden continued. "The transfer has been cleared through our judicial channels. This means that, provided our regulations concerning reimbursement of taxpayer expenses are met, along with a standard Party surcharge, and whatever staff gratuities you, as his release sponsor, deem appropriate, we can transfer the prisoner."

"How does that sound to you, Prisoner Smith?" Swan asked.

"Wonderful, sir," Winston said to the warden. He would have gotten on his knees and licked the man's boots if that would have got him out any sooner. "I am profoundly grateful for your . . . compassion."

"I shouldn't have to tell you that Compassionate Conservatism is a hallmark of our Administration," Swan said stiffly. Winston joined the warden and two Homeland Security prison guards in nodding their agreement. "Warden Moore, will you please enable the prisoner to effect a secure transfer?"

"Set him loose, men, and bring his chair to the desk," the warden said. He ordered his video monitor to face Winston, and dropped a security keyboard in front of him. He added some numbers to a paper that Neil Swan handed him, and set it in front of Winston.

"Prisoner Winston Smith, state your name, national ID number and the name of your bank," ordered the warden.

Winston did so. "Voice verification complete for Winston Smith," a pleasant voice from the computer stated. "Please look into the center of the screen for optic scan verification . . . Optical verification complete for Winston Smith. Please proceed with your transaction while looking into the center of the screen for continued authorization."

"Homeland Security Prison Services Corporation," Winston stated, reading from the paper in front of him. "Hullibarton, Bahamas Central Bank, account number WRG-47-62172, transfer four hundred thousand dollars. Nationalist Party Special Surcharge Account, Bahamas Central Bank, account number RL-82356, transfer two hundred thousand dollars."

"Funds transferred as requested," the computer replied politely.

"Neil L. Swan, Cayman Islands Heritage Bank, account NLS-32980, transfer one hundred fifty thousand dollars," Winston continued. "The Honorable Clarence Harding, Cayman Islands Heritage Bank, account CH-21093, transfer one hundred twenty thousand dollars. George R. Moore, Cayman Islands Heritage Bank account GRM-32901, transfer one hundred thousand dollars." Winston realized his mouth was dry.

"Funds transferred as requested," the computer confirmed.

"Please hold open for additional transfers," Winston requested. He turned away from the screen to the other men in the room. "I . . . I'll need additional names and accounts for the guard . . . gratuities."

"Prisoner Smith," Swan announced, "has volunteered to make additional gratuities to the personal accounts of the Homeland Security Services guards who provided such exemplary service during his short time here."

"I believe," the warden said, gesturing to the guard with the long scar across his neck, "that Nick Bartley was responsible for coordinating Prisoner Smith's welfare. Nick, could you please provide the prisoner with the form bearing the names and accounts of our guards."

"Prisoner Smith," Swan demanded. "What would you like to do for Officer Bartley?"

Nick dropped a form in front of Winston, who stared hard at a spot on the floor.

"Prisoner Smith," Swan demanded. "My copter's waiting and I've got to get back to the office, so don't space out on me again. Let's wind this up."

"Uhh . . . how does two hundred dollars sound?" Winston offered.

"Two hundred dollars? Did he say two hundred dollars?" Nick was agitated. "Boss, the money's not the issue, but could I speak to the prisoner alone for a few minutes, please, just two minutes alone?"

"No need, no need, Officer Bartley," Winston stammered. "Did I say two hundred dollars? I meant two hundred dollars an hour," Winston thought of the sadists waiting for him down the cellblock. His heart pounded. "What's that add up to—why don't we just say fifteen thousand dollars, and . . . and five thousand each of the other guards?"

Nick nodded. "Maybe you wants to make it an even twenty and ten?"

"Twenty thousand and ten thousand, of course, it's . . . a terrific suggestion," Winston said. He turned around and immediately read the names, account numbers and transfer amounts to the video screen.

"Done," Swan announced, lifting his massive frame out of the seat. He picked up a briefcase, and shook hands with Warden Moore and the two guards.

"Thank you, Warden, officers, for your help, and for seeing to it that the prisoner is transferred to the prison farm R-478, as detailed in his data file." Swan opened the door to leave. "Prisoner Smith, your new warden will be reporting to me on your calls to London," Swan warned Winston. "Cross us a second time, and you'll be back here before you can say, *Where are my laces?*"

The warden and guards laughed appreciatively.

"I won't disappoint you, Secretary Swan," Winston promised. "Thank you for coming today. You . . . you saved my life."

"Our Minister of Truth Russ Limetoff saved your life, Prisoner Smith," Neil concluded, standing by the door. "Don't forget it. Russ rewards loyalty, and he expects loyalty in return."

FOURTEEN

The sun had nearly set by the time Winston's prison van arrived at a large, well-lit sign announcing *Patriot Farms Site 12, Federal Prison Labor Camp*. High mesh fences topped with razor wire were posted with notices warning motorists that the area was patrolled with Predator drones, and that the unauthorized picking up of prisoners would result in the destruction of vehicles and the loss of life.

The van passed quickly through a fortified sentry gate, then drove for miles past fields of vegetables and melons, to a sprawling complex of more than two dozen squat cinderblock buildings, surrounded by scores of barrack-style tents. At the center of the complex was an industrial three-story operations building made of cement.

Guards dressed in dark blue paramilitary uniforms staffed the sentry station around the building's entrance. Winston was taken by the guard and driver from his van to the steps, where they were escorted into the building to a front office.

A clerk processed Winston's admission, while his guards entered a code into their controller device so they could remove his pain collar. Winston was ordered to speak and look at a camera, while his DNA, voice and optical data were downloaded onto the prison labor camp's central computer. Then his hand was placed in a device that fastened a data-encoded titanium bracelet to his wrist.

"This will be your only warning, so listen carefully," the clerk stated, bored. "Predator drones patrol the perimeter of this plantation. Should you attempt to leave at any time, you will be immediately destroyed, without notification. Sign and speak here that you understand, and forfeit all rights should you attempt to escape."

Winston signed and spoke his agreement. The guards brought him to a simply furnished waiting room nearby, locked him in, and left. Winston felt relieved as he watched, from a barred window, the van from the killing prison pull out.

A caravan of police vehicles, with lights flashing, arrived a few minutes later. A large blue logo across the side and back of the police cars read, *Patriot Farms Security*. Their motorcade led a huge armor-plated Hummer, equipped with gun ports and emergency lights.

Two bodyguards in paramilitary uniforms escorted out of the Hummer a tall, heavy-set man in a white and blue seersucker suit and Panama hat. He used a gold-tipped walking stick to slowly climb the building stairs.

A few minutes later, the man entered the waiting room and was seated near Winston. Although in his fifties and obese, the man's ostentatious style and apparent wealth lent him a dapper air. "Y'all can just wait outside," he said.

Two guards left and closed the door behind them.

"Welcome to Patriot Farms, Prisoner Smith," the man said, smiling broadly. "Mah name's Tex Watkins—heckuva name for a Florida boy, I guess it stuck wuth me cuz I'm so durned big."

"Thank you for accepting me into your facility, Warden Watkins . . ."

"Oh, ah ain't the warden, boy, ah'm the owner. And call me Mr. Watkins, boy, heck, just call me Mr. Tex. Everyone else does."

"I'm Winston Smith, sir, from New York, and very . . . grateful to be here."

"I know who you are, boy, that's what I'm doing heah. I got eighteen of these heah prison plantations. You think I greet every new arrival?"

"No, sir."

"Some very important people are paying special attention to you, boy." Tex pulled a fat cigar from his jacket and chomped on it as he looked Winston over. "I heah you reported directly to Neil Swan, Russ Limetoff's old drinking buddy, back in New York?"

"I did, sir. I hope to again one day."

"Ever meet the Minister of Truth himself?"

"A number of times, sir."

"What's Russ like, that fat old rascal?"

"Russ? A brilliant strategist, a loyal pillar of the Party and Administration."

"A man of sizable appetites, I heah," Tex said admiringly. "Likes his prescription oxy. And knows how to have a good time with the ladies." Tex winked slyly.

"I—I wouldn't know, sir. My role was purely professional, producing Homeland Security public service ads for video billboards."

"Each of us must do his part in the War on Terror," Tex agreed. He lit his cigar, inhaled contently, and let out a fat cloud of smoke. "Look at me. I house and feed and provide meaningful work for more than thirty two thousand inmates who violated their privilege to be free citizens. That's a lot of hungry mouths. It cost mucho millions to supply cots and dorms, especially starting out. But if we patriots neglected to answer General Bashcrost's call during Operation Clean Sweep, what would we have done with our nation's drug offenders?"

"It's the call of every Patriotic Citizen to do his duty to the Party," Winston said appreciatively, trying to work in as many Nationalist Party clichés as possible. "Freedom is never free."

"Mr. Tex," a guard interrupted, opening the door. "Your visitor wants—"

A beautiful, petite girl with caramel skin skipped through the door and bounced playfully onto Tex's lap. She was scarcely sixteen, and wore a very short summer dress, a garter, stockings, and spiked red high heels.

"Big Daddy, what you got for Kiera? " she said playfully, pinching his chest pockets. "Where's the tree?" she tittered. Oblivious to Winston's presence, she dug her hands inside his pants. "Where's Kiera's tree?"

"Oh, you sassy little devil," Tex laughed good-heartedly, adjusting his thick legs for comfort. "Detention coming right up for you, young lady." He smacked her bottom affectionately. "Now you just git right on up to my office. Ask Sergeant Crane to let you in. Just gimme ten more minutes. Thet's an order, young lady!"

"Yes sir, Mr. Tex," Kiera said coyly. "I'll be waiting," she ran out, shutting the door behind her.

"Ah, misled youth!" Tex exclaimed, biting his lip in anticipation. "That little girl had actually arranged to murder her unborn baby. Luckily, it was with an undercover operative who was part of General Bashcrost's national anti-abortion network."

Winston nodded his approval, thinking to himself, *What a fucking pig!*

"She threw herself at the mercy of the court," Tex continued, in a concerned, parental tone. "Underage and ignorant child. The court took mercy, and she was sentenced heah, to have her baby and serve out a reduced fifteen-year sentence."

"A lucky girl," Winston agreed.

"She could have faced execution for conspiracy to murder an unborn child. But Compassionate Conservatism is a hallmark of this Administration," Tex said. "Poor girl had no daddy, her mammy's poor as a church mouse. She gets special consideration heah, as one of my personal charity cases. Meanwhile, her baby was adopted by a good Christian family with . . . considerable resources," he grinned. "We're not vengeful here at Patriot Farms. Justice is our obligation, hand in hand with patriotism, and service to God's will, as interpreted by our great Commander in Chief, George O. Blush: A great leader, a great uniter, a great patriot!"

"A great leader, a great uniter, a great patriot," Winston repeated the Party response.

"Now with good behavior," Tex winked lasciviously and moved his fat face closer to Winston's, "and I tell you she behaves real good—Kiera's sentence can be cut by a third. She'll be out in just ten years, ready to become a good Christian mother!"

"Lucky she found you," Winston replied.

"A lot of us are lucky, thanks to God's grace. Praise the Lord!"

"Praise the Lord," Winston replied automatically.

"See, I'm not a complainer," Tex continued. "I do well, and the Party does well." He fingered an ornate insignia on his lapel, a design of the letter "P" in small diamonds. "You know how much a Patriotic Citizen has to donate to the Party these days to be a Senior Pioneer, boy?"

Winston knew, but replied, "No, sir. How much?"

"One million dollars for the Party, per year, then another million dollars consulting fees for state party officials, then another million consulting fees for national party officials. Do the math."

"Whew," Winston pretended to be impressed. "That's a pretty penny."

"Dammed right it is. Three million a year! But don't get me wrong. My eighteen farms and thirty-two thousand inmates earn me that much profit every few days." Tex puffed proudly on his cigar. "I ain't no hymie whiner. The Party has a right to our financial support. It cut taxes, got regulation off our back. Free enterprise made this country great."

"And Patriotic Citizens must never allow skeptics to drag it down," Winston recited the Party's follow-up slogan.

Tex grinned, duly impressed. "It's a shame when a boy of your understanding strays," he said, puffing on the cigar. "While we're on the subject of money, I understand that you're able to pay your way, unlike some of the deadbeats around here?"

"That's right, sir."

"Good. Some of the prisoners heah think they can coast on their work alone. Let's just say they don't eat too well, don't get much sleep in their sweaty tents, and that fifty hours is only half their work week." Tex's belly bounced as he laughed at his clever characterization.

"Fair is fair," Winston said.

"Let me bring you a secure computer and we'll get this money part over with." Tex hit a button on his phone. "Elvis," he commanded, "bring a banking computer in heah."

A towering, broad-shouldered man with a thick dark handlebar moustache entered, carrying a small computer. He wore a black leather motorcycle jacket with *Patriot Farms Security* patches on both arms, captain bars on the shoulders, and a lawman's badge over the chest. Two western-style pearl-handled revolvers hung from a bullet-studded belt low around his waist. The man set the computer on a table near Winston and tapped a button. A monitor folded out, and a three-dimensional keyboard appeared on the table.

"This heah's Elvis," Tex announced. "He's the warden of Patriot Farms Site 12, the guardian of the two thousand two hundred souls entrusted to our care while working off their federal transgressions. Whatever he says is law."

"I understand you want A-class accommodations and food," Elvis declared.

"That's right," Winston replied.

"It's seven hundred dollars a day, twenty-one thousand a month," Elvis said. "We'll need automatic transfer authority on a monthly basis, payable in advance. Here's the wire transfer data."

Winston called out his bank account. The computer performed a voice and optic verification. It took less than a minute more to arrange the transfer and monthly payments.

"Part one of our business is done," Tex stated, eager to finish up and get to his office. "You got a phone on that, don't you?" he asked Elvis.

"'Course we do, boss."

"Mute the video," Tex ordered the computer. "Distribute secure copies of the recording to my central office, Neil Swan at the Ministry of Truth in New York, and the Site 12 local file."

"As requested, Mr. Tex," a pleasant voice from the computer replied. "What number would you like to call?"

"Prisoner Smith," Tex commanded, "get your friend Paul Goode from the BBC on the line. You know what you need to do."

FIFTEEN

Winston recited Paul's number from memory. The computer dialed it.

"Hello," Paul answered, sounding irritated at being woken up. It was past three a.m. in London.

"Paul, it's Winston."

"Winston," Paul's voice grew serious and concerned. "Lilly called me right after you didn't show up at the airport. Are you okay?"

"Yes," Winston replied, barely able to keep himself from falling apart. "I was arrested at JFK and convicted of subversive behavior by a Homeland Security Court, for selling my script to the BBC. I'm in a prison labor camp as we speak."

"Uh-huh . . ." Paul replied, cautiously.

"I was originally sentenced to ultimate rehabilitation at a Special Homeland Security prison for my offense—"

"You were sentenced to ultimate rehabilitation for what you did here in London?" Paul sounded incredulous.

"Affirmative," Winston continued. He could tell that Paul

understood this meant a death sentence. "You can imagine my relief when I was told that I could be transferred to the prison labor camp that I am currently calling you from, on one condition."

"I'm listening . . ."

"I need to convince the BBC to cancel the project. I need your help with this. I can help pay for costs incurred to date."

"Winston, I do not control everything the BBC does."

"Please, Paul," Winston struggled to maintain his composure. "I cannot emphasize how serious this is. I made a huge mistake. This is a matter of life or death."

Paul was silent for a moment. "It's three in the morning. I need to think . . . of the best way to approach this, internally. I . . . I'll need some time."

"Of course. I should be able to call you again in a few days. Next time at a more reasonable hour."

"Call anytime. Please, Winston . . . take care of yourself."

"I . . ." Winston held back a torrent of tears. "You know me—I'll try to make the best of it. Thank you so much, Paul."

After Winston got off the phone, he took a moment to breathe deeply.

"It's a start," Tex said, unimpressed. "You'll need to keep on it, until your objective is accomplished. The warden will arrange access for the calls."

Tex looked toward the door. "Now you'll have ta excuse a horny old goat," he grinned, gathering the energy to lift his body off the chair. "I got a lovely gal waiting for her Big Daddy."

"Thank you, Mr. Tex, for your . . . hospitality."

Tex started slowly for the doorway, then turned around. "Play the Party for a fool," he warned, "and it will be the last game you ever play."

Elvis escorted Winston out of the building and through the hall of a nearby cinderblock dormitory. Winston was surprised by an absence of gates, sentry points, locks, or even cell doors.

Inmates passed along the hall, moving freely in casual attire. The inmates were a wide mix of races and ages, many with long hair, a good number with dreadlocks. It was evening, and people were socializing, watching video, playing cards, listening to music, reading. The atmosphere reminded Winston of a low-rent college dorm he had visited while in England a decade earlier.

They arrived in the doorway of a room with two cots, one bare and the other occupied by a man stretched out, reading. Soul music played soothingly from a portable stereo, and a ceiling fan kept the warm air moving. The cinderblock walls had been painted with the bright red, green and black colors of the Pan-African movement. Books, paper and journals overflowed a small desk, dresser and file cabinet.

The warden cleared his throat loudly. The room's occupant stirred, sat up in the bed, and swatted his forehead in frustration. He was a tall, African-American man in his fifties, with dreadlocks and light freckles. Despite the sweatpants and Bob Marley tee shirt he wore, the man still managed to look distinguished.

"Heads up, Professor. I need to introduce you to your new roomie. Winston Smith, meet Professor Malcolm Jefferson." The man watched them from his bed, irritated. Elvis handed Winston a plastic bag he had been carrying, and recited his standard welcome. "This contains a portable A-ration meal for your dinner, and a prison manual for accommodation level A. It'll tell you everything you need to know. Read all the rules, you're required to know and abide by them from day one. Your plantation identity tag is your bracelet, don't ever try to take it off. You'll need it for entry into the cafeteria at mealtimes. The night shift orderly will bring your work clothes and bedding in a little while."

Malcolm bounced up from his bed and stood eye to eye with the warden. "Yo, Elvis my man," he said, in a friendly tone. "Tell me what is going on here? I'm supposed to have a private room for six months if I paid extra. I paid extra."

"We're full up in Class A, Professor. Gotta change the deal."

Elvis shrugged. "Hope you enjoyed it while it lasted."

"Five days? That ain't six months! What's the real deal? You need a spy, just drop a few more bugs in here and leave me my six months. Don't make me live with a snitch, Elvis. Gimme a break . . ."

"He ain't no snitch, we're full up, so now we can't make exceptions for single rooms, it's as simple as that. You'll get credit for the privacy surcharge. My hands are tied, man."

"Elvis, c'mon. This is Malcolm you're talking to. You the warden, you the man. I know you can find some space for that rich white kid somewhere else."

"I gotta do what I gotta do, Professor. Look, nothing says you gotta talk to the dude. Just bring him to the crew leader in the morning. He'll figure the rest out."

"I'd be glad to take a different room," Winston offered.

Elvis turned on him like an attack dog. "Shut the fuck up, Smith. You'll stay where you're told. The only other room we got is in the tents, and an office boy like you would die in the summer heat in one'a them. Then what would happen to next month's rent?" Elvis laughed and pointed Winston toward the empty cot in the room. "You sleep there. I'll collect you Thursday at seven for your next phone call. If you're not here, it's hot box solitaire."

Elvis disappeared down the hallway. Malcolm returned to his cot, turned his back to Winston, and resumed reading.

Winston sat on his cot, ripped open his ration box, and ate ravenously. The portion was ample and after a week of D-rations, tasted delicious. He was still surprised that there was no door to the room. "Can we just walk in and out whenever we want?"

"You can do whatever the fuck you want," Malcolm replied, tersely. He stormed out of the room and down the hall.

Three days passed. Malcolm had not said a single word to Winston. They were far off in a field just a hundred yards from the perimeter gates, part of a ten-person work crew, all of them kneeling in the rich, well-irrigated earth, transplanting thousands of small melon seedlings from the greenhouse. Malcolm labored silently down the row from Winston. It was eleven in the morning and the Florida sun was scorching hot. Winston's shirt was soaked with sweat. He had gone through his first gallon of water, so he walked up the row to refill his jug from the cart.

An open pickup truck came tearing up the tractor trail near the water cart. As it came to a screeching halt, two taut, hungry-looking Hispanic men raced to it from the field near the perimeter fence.

"We got the gate cut wide open!" the faster of the escaping inmates yelled to Winston, excitedly, as he leapt into the back of the truck. It was driven by a well-dressed accomplice who had entered the camp as a visitor. The second inmate was running toward them, still twenty paces from the truck.

Winston's heart pounded and his mind raced. He was scheduled to make his second call to Paul that evening. Paul might tell him that it was impossible for the BBC to stop the film. Winston would then be transferred back to the killing prison. Maybe the truck could get out of Predator drone range before their escape registered?

Winston noted that he was as close to the back of the escape truck as the second inmate. He looked across the field and could see the cut-open section of the fence.

A heavy hand grabbed his shoulder, so unexpectedly that Winston jumped as he spun around. It was Malcolm.

"Do not follow them," Malcolm's voice was strong and hypnotically clear. "That way lies your death. Drones don't miss."

Winston froze in his tracks. The second inmate sprinted over the back into the truck. It shot into high gear instantly. The escaping men never looked back.

The sky was clear blue and there was not a sound save the truck racing full speed through the gap in the fence. The truck reached the paved road outside the prison fence. It turned sharply and gained speed as it raced to the left. From nowhere, two drones arrived. They hovered effortlessly in the air, quickly moving into position, tracking the front and back of the pickup truck. The day erupted with two huge blasts of fire and noise. Flames flew fifty feet into the air.

Malcolm stared solemnly at Winston. Sadness swelled in his eyes. "We better get back to work," he said, suddenly seeming very wise.

SIXTEEN

The Predator drones hovered silently in the air, guarding the hole in the prison plantation's fence until a Patriot Farms police van arrived to repair it. Malcolm and Winston returned to work. Under the watchful cameras of the drones, Malcolm was careful not to say too much.

Later in the day, as they ate an early dinner in the cafeteria, Malcolm sat down next to Winston for the first time since his arrival.

"I should let you save my life more often," Winston joked, "if that's what it takes to get you to speak to me."

"I hear you've got an important phone call tonight?" Malcolm asked.

Winston had the sense that after eight years at the labor camp, Malcolm knew everything that was going on. "I've been dreading it since I got here. This place may not be great, but it sure beats where I came from. How much do you know?"

"Enough to offer a few words of advice," Malcolm said.

Malcolm looked around to make sure there was plenty of noise at their crowded cafeteria table. He spoke in short spurts while taking forkfulls of food into his mouth and loudly chewing.

"Talk over me about the food . . . listen while you talk," he advised.

Winston began making small talk.

"Your friend . . ." Malcolm chewed and wiped his mouth. ". . . he knows you'll be killed if the movie is made . . . but he can't lie to you because BBC is filled with bugs and informers . . . don't seem disappointed . . . don't demand results . . . give him time."

At exactly seven p.m., the warden appeared in Winston's doorway. He brought Winston to the operations building, into a room where inmates rented phone time.

"Can I keep the video on this time?" Winston asked. He wanted Paul to see that he was unharmed, and to tell Lilly that he was still in one piece. He had considered asking for a phone call home, but he knew that he would need to show results from his BBC calls before asking for new privileges.

The warden agreed, knowing that Homeland Security always appreciated video footage of foreign journalists. Paul prudently kept the camera turned off from his end.

"Unfortunately, it's going to take a while to process my request," Paul explained. "A meeting is scheduled for next week. I'll need to work my way through the proper channels to get the project cancelled. Remember, *1984* has been on their schedule for a long time. So I don't want to jump to the top right away. Although we might get a fast *yes* that way, it might also result in a fast *no*, and I don't want to risk that."

"That's . . . encouraging," Winston said carefully. It had been four days since his desperate request. Paul knew his life depended on it. How could he be so casual about this? Then Winston recalled Malcolm's advice, forced a smile and added, "You know how best to navigate those bureaucratic BBC waters."

They scheduled another call for the following week, after

Paul's meeting. The warden sent Winston back to his dormitory.

Malcolm was waiting for him. "How'd it go?" he asked.

Winston shrugged, unsure.

"Want to take a walk?" Malcolm offered.

"A . . . walk?"

"Sure, kid. It's allowed, long as you don't leave the grounds. You saw what happens when you do."

They walked out into the warm north Florida air. Malcolm led him up a farm road, through a field, and down an irrigation trail. Finally, more than a mile from their dormitory, he sat down against a tree.

"Isn't there a curfew?" Winston asked, sitting next to him. "I mean, it's past nine."

"Hey, man, this here's free enterprise. We're Class A inmates, which to Mr. Tex means big bucks. Pay in advance, give them fifty hours of hard labor, stay within the fence, and just about anything goes. Pay extra, and there are few things you can't buy."

Malcolm pulled a hand-rolled cigarette out of his pocket, lit it, and inhaled deeply.

"Is that what I think it is?" Winston asked, smelling high-quality marijuana.

Malcolm held his breath, nodded, and passed the joint to Winston. Winston turned it down.

"I didn't expect you to say yes," Malcolm said, exhaling "It was months before I realized it was cool to buy and smoke reefer here. Elvis's men sell some mean sens. And it sure helps the days pass."

"Elvis—the warden?"

"I imagine he gives the plantation owner a share," Malcolm replied, taking another toke. "Tex has his hand in everything. More than a little ironic though, since marijuana in my blood is what sent me here for ten fucken years."

"When was that?"

Malcolm suddenly became agitated. "When do you think? Remember Operation Clean Sweep, from Election Day 2006?"

"You got . . . swept up in that?" Winston recalled, with some guilt, how he had supported the move at the time as helpful to national security. That was the first time his boss Neil Swan had used the cliché "You can't make an omelet without breaking eggs."

Malcolm spat on the ground nearby. He took another toke and shook his head slowly. "Me and twenty million other former citizens of this great racist country. Our crime was showing up in polling places that had demonstrated a pattern of Democratic and alternative party voting. They herded us into side rooms, and instantly tested us for residue of illegal drugs. You know weed shows up in the hair for months?"

Winston nodded. Malcolm held out what was left of his joint. "This helps keep my blood pressure down when I get angry."

"You . . . strike me as a calm person," Winston suggested.

"I try to live with my anger. Ten year mandatory felony sentence for marijuana in the blood possession, with no parole, was part of the federal Zero Tolerance Bill of 2006. You remember how hard Blush and Bashcrost pushed for it, and how it squeaked through a divided Congress early that year? Nobody thought it'd be applied, just another crazy War on Drugs law for the books."

Malcolm looked at the stars, took a breath to calm down, and continued. "Then the Scaria Supreme Court, in what they called an emergency ruling brought on by the drug crisis, upheld selective application of the law by the D.E.A. and F.B.I.—meaning at roadblocks in African-American and Latino neighborhoods and near college campuses. Then on Election Day, local police, state police, D.E.A. and F.B.I. agents, U.S. Army, even the National Guard and National Reserve were called out to test, arrest and transport all of us who showed up to vote in that fucken congressional election. It took years in jam-packed internment camps before their fatcat cronies could build enough factory labor camps and plantations to house us all. And you can be sure that very few black folks, college liberals or young Latinos showed up for the 2008 presidential elections."

"Didn't it help cut down on crime?" Winston asked half-heartedly, recalling the Nationalist Party response to the huge public outcry that resulted.

"Cut crime?" Malcolm shot back. "Shit, they created criminals. And reduced the voting population in most minority neighborhoods to almost nothing overnight. That's how they completed their takeover of the government! But hell, everybody knows that."

Like most Nationalist Party members at the time, Winston had regarded the decimation of the Democratic Party in America as a convenient by-product of Operation Clean Sweep—and he had celebrated it with his Nationalist friends. He even supported the judicial recall movement promoted by Russ Limetoff and Bob O'Manley those years, to recall "activist" judges who refused to support aspects of search and seizure provisions of Patriot Act III and Operation Clean Sweep.

Winston himself had stopped smoking marijuana and switched to hard liquor as soon as the Zero Tolerance legislation was announced. He recalled how General Bashcrost had responded to questioning during the televised 2007 congressional hearings investigating Operation Clean Sweep. "We're just enforcing the law!" he had yelled angrily. "Why is it that you Democrats always insist on coddling criminals?"

Winston felt the sting of shame. But what choice had there been back then? By 2007, he was already working in the communications arm of the Administration. Nobody could have expected him to bite the powerful hand that fed him.

He decided to change the subject. "So how do you afford it all in here," Winston asked. "I mean, the A-class accommodations, the reefer?"

"Fortunately, my wife Clarita has a good job as a pharmaceutical rep." Malcolm seemed eager to change the subject as well, and think of his family. He took a long toke and blew rings of smoke. "She's a kickass saleswoman, makes decent money.

Basically, she sends most of it here. And our two kids help a little."

"You must miss her," Winston said, thinking fondly of Lilly. How long had it been since he had seen her? A month or more?

"Oh, she visits every couple of months," Malcolm explained. "Conjugal visits. They got a special love motel in one of the dorms. Special price list for that, too."

They laughed, and continued talking until well past midnight.

Winston was tired when they woke early for work the next morning. But he slept during the midday break, and by the next evening, he was ready for another walk.

Malcolm brought Winston to a different sitting spot every night, determined to avoid having their conversations bugged.

For years, Winston had managed to filter out inconvenient facts about the government he worked for. As advised, he had dismissed dissidents as losers, whiners, Subversives, and unworthy citizens. But unlike other dissidents Winston had met during his life, Malcolm was able to eloquently articulate his objections to the Blush Administration's policies, and to back up his arguments with disturbing facts and statistics. Malcolm had been an investigative journalist and journalism professor, and teaching came naturally to him. Winston listened and learned.

In the face of Malcolm's senseless incarceration and his own recent experiences, Winston's role as a propagandist for the Homeland Security Department, and the enthusiasm he had once brought to his advancement in Nationalist Party circles, now only brought embarrassment. But he needed to speak with someone, and after a while, he came clean.

Within a few weeks, Winston had told Malcolm about his father's death, his subsequent political conversion at the age of seventeen, his mother's flight to Costa Rica to join other dissidents, his career, his *1984* project, and all the changes that were taking place in his thinking since his transformative experience in London.

He began to feel close to Malcolm. He was surprised when,

during one of their periodic talks Malcolm suddenly brought a small cloth bag from his pocket and pulled out a small electronic bug detector.

"Just need to be sure," Malcolm said, moving the device carefully across every part of Winston's body. "Please pick up your feet, slowly, one at a time."

SEVENTEEN

Winston complied with Malcolm's request, uneasily. "Why . . . where'd you get that?" he asked.

"I told you that money can buy anything in this place," Malcolm replied. "As for why . . . your recent true confessions got me worrying. You worked for some powerful people, and they're keeping a close eye on you. Just wanted to make sure that eye wasn't extending itself to me . . . you're clean."

Winston sat down, relieved. "I understand. I'm glad to hear there are no bugs on me, after tonight's call. I wanted to talk to you about it."

"What happened?"

"Nothing happened," Winston explained. "That's the problem. It's been three weeks, and I can't tell if Paul is getting anywhere with the higher-ups at the BBC. It just seems to be meetings, more meetings, and waiting for meetings. I thought that once they understood my life depended on it, they'd pull their *1984* project."

"Unfortunately, you're not the first person threatened with

death if the BBC doesn't back down. Between the fundamentalists' fatwa, death threats by crony governments in American-occupied countries, and our government's own murderous war on international dissent, this sort of shit happens more often than you can imagine."

"How did things get so fucked up?" Winston asked.

"You know what Edmund Burke said, back when this country was starting out: 'All that is required for evil to prevail is for good men to do nothing.' The Blush gang used their unending War on Terror as an excuse to make sure good folks are no longer *able* to do anything. I used to tell my students it was this government's 'National Insecurity State' strategy. I'd be jailed for saying that today. They've now fired or imprisoned every professor and teacher who wouldn't join the Nationalist Party, labeling them Subversive, or traitorous. Remember, right after 9-11, when Susan Sontag warned about the lobotomizing effect of a war without end?"

"It's funny," Winston said, thinking about his screenplay adaptation. "In a way that's what *1984* is about."

"'Course it is," Malcolm continued. "There's a reason they don't want that movie made. To the Blush government, the whole War on Terror has been just one large excuse to consolidate political power and crush reasonable debate and political dissent."

"You make it seem like one big conspiracy," Winston said, thinking of the mostly well-mannered professionals he had worked with in the Party. "I always saw it as a bunch of people, some of them insensitive, who believe they're patriots working to keep the country safe, maybe sometimes over-reacting."

"That's one way to look at it," Malcolm said, lighting a joint and smoking it slowly. "Just a bunch of well-intentioned white folk trying to make the world safe for democracy. Problem is you can't destroy democracy to preserve it. You don't need to destroy the free press, jail and execute dissenters, outlaw opposition parties, bankrupt the economy to pay for military spending and tax cuts for the wealthy, throw twenty million citizens into crony-run for-profit prison labor camps, kill millions of innocent civilians in Pakistan, Indonesia, Egypt, Syria and Iran, install dictators with paramilitary death squads to run puppet governments in countries we occupy, destroy all relationships with every ally in the developed world, not to mention the authority of the United Nations . . . you don't need to do all this to fight terrorism."

"Whew," Winston grinned. "That was a mouthful. Feel better now?"

Malcolm smiled and took another hit of the joint.

"Some people would say that our government has its reasons?"

"Profits and political power," Malcolm said, with certainty. "You think that Operation Traitor Recall had anything to do with national security?"

"It seemed to at the time," Winston replied, embarrassed to say more. Operation Traitor Recall was, in fact, his first major campaign with Neil Swan and Russ Limetoff soon after he joined the communications effort of the Blush Administration. Winston had just moved from a journalism career at Foxy News to a job producing political ads for the Nationalist Party's enormous, well-funded effort to recall liberal politicians in nearly all fifty states. In order to revoke term limits for President Blush and allow him to run in the 2008 presidential elections, state legislatures across the country needed to ratify a congressional amendment, but a number of politicians had openly opposed it.

It had been Russ Limetoff's brilliant idea to use each of Foxy's local stations to promote the Nationalist Party's Operation Traitor Recall. First came the polls that asked, "Do you think that traitorous politicians who refuse to give President George Blush the power he needs to fight the War on Terror ought to be allowed to remain in office?" Paid Nationalist Party workers fanned out across the states to gather names on recall petitions. Foxy News kept the tallies of signatories running continually, and proclaimed the recall elections to be "the single most important weapon this country has in its war against terror." Hundreds of state legislators, dozens of congressmen, and even five governors were defeated in recalls, and by 2008, two thirds of Congress and a majority of state legislators had passed the 28th Amendment. The amendment, Winston recalled, set the groundwork for Blush's landslide reelection to a third term, during which he was able to get the support required to replace the Constitution with a Patriotic Citizen's Bill of Rights.

"Hey Winston," Malcolm snapped his fingers. "Where are you?"

Winston's stomach felt queasy. It seemed like someone else's past. "I was part of it then, y'know," he admitted.

"I guessed as much," Malcolm said.

"They weren't traitors, those politicians who got recalled," Winston buried his face in his hands and rubbed his eyes hard. "They were opponents of the Administration. We ruined them. It was all about power—and money. My bonus when the term limit amendment passed was double my salary that year. I was deep in that shit, Malcolm, deep in it."

"Never too late for a happy childhood," Malcolm advised, looking at the night sky full of stars.

As the summer arrived, the Florida sun became relentless, and the inmates' work schedule changed. They started earlier, broke well before noon, then returned to the fields for a few hours before dark.

Winston made his weekly calls to Paul at midday, always with the same conclusion: "They're considering it . . . no decision made yet . . . another meeting in a few days."

At the beginning of his second and third month, Winston made a point of asking for the warden's account number and transferring generous gratuities for his assistance in making the important calls.

"You could stay here fifty years, for all I care," the warden said to him, after Winston paid for his third month in advance, along with a two thousand dollar gratuity. "Hell, more money for me. But it ain't up to me. If the Party doesn't see results real soon . . ." the warden's voice trailed off.

Winston woke that night in a cold sweat, dreaming of the violence and murderous taunts of the killers in the Homeland Security special prison.

The next day, he and Malcolm worked the late afternoon shift in a field far from their dormitory. As they harvested watermelons and laid them in huge crates for pickup, he noticed a vehicle kicking up a trail of dust as it headed their way. He wondered whether the Patriot Farms security force was coming to pick him up and transfer him back to the killing prison. He felt a sudden urge to run, to climb the fence and let the drones blow him apart.

Malcolm seemed to read his mind. "Chill," he advised knowingly. "It's probably just a truck picking up the melons."

Winston relaxed as soon as a mid-sized tractor-trailer, and not a paramilitary vehicle, came into view. It raced up the trail to where they had been filling crates with watermelons, then came to a screeching halt, kicking up a cloud of dirt.

A young woman climbed down from the driver's seat. Her short green hair was trimmed to a marine-style crew cut, and the well-worked muscles in her old sleeveless tee shirt made Winston wonder whether she was in fact a Marine. But as she walked closer, Winston noticed four rings through her pierced eyebrow, and another one through her nose. She wore loose cargo pants with a knife sheathed in her belt. Although scarcely out of her teens, she had the weathered, road-warrior look of a truck driver who had been doing speed to compensate for a week of sleepless nights.

"Is your name Dawn?" Malcolm asked.

"Dawn has indeed arrived," the girl announced. She stooped over, clenched her hands together behind her back, and stretched her limber arms behind her in a yoga pose. The move revealed the top of a huge colored tattoo of the yin and yang symbol, with a serpent swimming through it that seemed to stretch across the whole of her back. "Damn, that was a long drive," she said. "I take it you're Malcolm?"

Malcolm nodded, and quickly looked around to make sure nobody else could see them. The field was clear of people and vehicles for as far as his eyes could see.

"This must be the special cargo," Dawn said, pointing to Winston. "How much does he know?"

"Know about what?" Winston looked at Malcolm, baffled and indignant at being kept in the dark.

"Nothing," Dawn observed, answering her own question. "Good."

A tall, lanky boy got out of the passenger side of the truck, and loudly slid open the back of the trailer. He climbed in, and emerged down a ramp a few seconds later driving a forklift.

"We gotta load this sucker up and move," he said, as he drove past the others and scooped up a watermelon-filled crate. His arms were so skinny they looked as though they might break off at any moment, but he operated the lift with speed and skill. He appeared to be part Asian, part Hispanic, and too young to have a driver's license. He brought the lift to a stop near the ramp and walked up next to Dawn.

"This is Quinn," Dawn said, introducing the boy. Three silver spikes protruded through his chin, one ear was covered with tiny rings, and he periodically stuck his pierced tongue out to flick a small screwed-in computer chip stud against his strangely-filed front teeth, making a light, steady tapping sound. A tattoo of a lock and chain circled his neck, and disappeared down his back. He eyed Winston curiously.

"We're replacing a legit truck run, " Dawn said, "So we gotta fill the belly with watermelons. It shouldn't take more than twenty minutes if Quinn handles the crates and we fill the aisle with loose melons. There's a hidden, secure space for you two in the far back of the trailer. Quinn's team has made a jammer for your prison bracelets that should fool the drones."

Quinn pulled two small electronic devices from a pocket and showed them off in his palm. "Check it out. It's a G.P.S. jam, man! Our Info Tech unit rigged it up special for you."

"We activate that thing," Dawn explained, "It'll read your DNA, just like the transmitter in the bracelet it emulates—"

"It doesn't actually emulate the bracelet signal," Quinn interjected. "It—"

"Whatever!" Dawn scolded, in a tone like an older sister. "I'm in charge of this action, Quinn, I do the explaining."

"Sorry."

"Anyway," Dawn continued, "it sends a false signal telling the global positioning satellite that you're safe within the prison zone, no matter where you are. By the time they figure out you're gone and reverse engineer Quinn's brilliant fix, we'll have completed a secure removal from home base and made the bracelet disappear."

"No fingerprints in cyberspace!" Quinn boasted, pleased that she had called his invention brilliant, waving his bony fingers. Tribal patterns were tattooed like thick rings around most of the fingers. "Info Tech's gonna hook you dudes up big time!"

"We can't just drive outta here with some untested gizmo on our prison bracelets," Winston protested. "Those drones don't ask questions."

"Dude, hows 'bout a little faith in I.T.?" Quinn complained.

"But your . . . unit . . . never tried this before?"

"So? There's lots of shit that works the first time, right out of the lab."

"Yeah? Well, there's probably more shit that fucks up the first time. And if you're wrong, the drones will make this truck a crematorium for all four of us."

"Suit yourself, dude," Quinn shrugged. "We all gotta go sometime."

Quinn got back on the forklift, drove up the ramp, stacked the watermelon crate in the truck, and sped out for another load.

"I appreciate your coming to help me," Winston told Dawn.

"But why should I risk the drones and be on the run forever when there's a chance I might be coasting out of here on my own steam before long?"

"Because the BBC has already made a decision to begin production on *1984* next week," Dawn replied.

Winston felt like the wind had been knocked out of him. "What do you know about—"

"If we didn't know nothing," Dawn explained, "we wouldn't be here right now. Then the only ride you'd be taking tonight would be your 'ultimate rehabilitation.' Lucky for you, your pal Paul is connected. He's been a Resistance International member since I started—and I started young. Works with our cell, among others, has London hackers e-mail independent info, documentary video, and foreign Resistance communication to our offshore remote e-mail boxes, which we pick up through untraceable slave servers. He helps sneak truth in between the cracks, which is the only place we can get any these days. He sent us to save your ass."

Quinn's forklift rushed past with another huge crate of melons and Dawn looked at her watch. Winston noticed how alluring her hazel-colored eyes were when she wasn't squinting.

"But Paul has influence with the BBC," Winston protested. "He's worked there for—"

"The BBC decision was made internally yesterday. They're keeping it real private, but General Bashcrost has people everywhere, and production begins in a week. Paul figured he had two days before the leak sprung. Trust me on this: you stick around here, you're toast."

Winston looked at the titanium bracelet on his wrist, then at Malcolm. "What do you think?"

"I understand at least two things," Malcolm said carefully. "First is that the Resistance never bullshits. Second is that when you fuck with the Party, unless they've got some use for you, you're dead. And so am I, if you escape and I'm left behind. In the end, it's your call."

"Look, I know it's a big decision," Dawn said. "Whatever you decide, we're gonna have to fill this sucker with watermelons and deliver them to Bed-Stuy whether you join us or not. Why don't you help load it up while you think it over?"

Winston thought it over while the four of them worked quickly to load and distribute the heavy crates in the trailer, then top them off with more melons. Dawn guided the sweaty work as they nearly filled the aisle with loose-stacked melons, leaving just enough space along the top of the aisle for a person to crawl through to the back.

Each time Winston walked down the trailer ramp to haul up more melons, he looked across the long empty fields, worried that security vehicles would be coming to get him. He slowly got his mind to trust the tiny devices to fool the drones. But what was even more difficult was accepting that he would never return to the powerful fold of the Party, to his job, his apartment, his prestige.

Malcolm walked up next to him while he paused at the bottom of the ramp. "Change is never easy," Malcolm said. "But sometimes essential."

Quinn whirred past with his last forklift load, and parked it at the back of the trailer. Dawn waved him down to where Winston and Malcolm were standing.

"You'll need to climb through to get to the back compartment," Quinn explained. "Dawn and I will block it up behind you."

"Decision time, Mr. Smith," Dawn said. "You staying or going?"

"Going," Winston said. "Let's get the fuck outta here."

"Right choice," Dawn agreed, "assuming you wanna keep living."

Quinn attached the tiny electronic devices he had brought to Winston and Malcolm's prison security bracelets, then pressed the activation key on a controller he carried. The devices stirred, emitted light beeps, then fell silent. Quinn looked at his controller and seemed satisfied with the reading.

"So here's the skinny," Dawn explained. "Close the sliding panel to the compartment once you get in it. There'll be a tiny light in there, and a couple of sleeping bags and pads. You can talk to each other as long as the truck is moving, but you gotta stay completely silent anytime we slow down or stop. No movement, no whispers, statue-like, okay?"

"What if—" Winston began.

"No what-ifs on this ride," Dawn interjected. "It's out of your hands, at this point. Trust in Jah, trust in fate, trust in whatever you believe in. Just don't make the slightest fucken sound when we stop. Okay, there's a gallon of water in there, and here's a shank to cut up all the watermelon you can eat." Dawn handed Malcolm the long knife that hung from the sheath on her waist.

"Got it," Malcolm agreed, tucking the knife in his waist.

Winston and Malcolm climbed awkwardly on top of an aisle of melons that didn't quite reach the ceiling of the trailer, and made their way to a narrow opening at the back. They climbed through the opening in the false wall, and closed the hidden panel behind them.

They heard the back of the trailer roll shut. The engine started, and punk music blasted from the front seat, as the truck lurched forward across the field.

EIGHTEEN

The truck drove slowly on the bumpy field. It stopped at the prison camp's main gate as a sentry checked the driver's papers. A gate opened, and the truck picked up speed as it headed toward the highway.

A tiny yellow light glowed in the small compartment where Winston and Malcolm hid, each of them perched on a watermelon for a rough seat. Winston heard the sound of a drone hovering nearby. He spoke quietly to Malcolm. "Whatever happens, thank you for risking your life for me. I . . . I can't say I would have done the same."

Malcolm smiled uneasily. He could hear the drone hovering overhead, too. "We do what we're called on. But you're welcome." Malcolm closed his eyes and lost himself in prayer.

Winston looked at the device on his bracelet and prayed that the patch would work. The seconds dragged slowly.

Malcolm wiped the sweat that had formed on his brow.

Winston watched him, and after a few minutes, smiled. "It worked!" he said.

"That was the first test," Malcolm replied, relieved. "Let's hope the other patches help us make it to Bed-Stuy undetected."

The truck lurched from an entry ramp onto a highway and loudly picked up speed. Winston slipped off the large watermelon he was sitting on and fell to the floor.

Malcolm helped him up. "This compartment," he said, "may not be designed for comfort, but it's technologically more advanced than you'd think."

Winston adjusted his body. "Very clever," he agreed. "I'm sure not many cops would move thirty feet of watermelons stacked eight feet high to get to the back of the truck."

"A major sentry checkpoint would never be fooled just by that. Homeland Security has equipment to detect anything: body heat, radiation, explosives, traces of chemical or biological agents. The challenge is to mask our heat-generating bodies."

"I hope it works," Winston said.

"They got us past the drones," Malcolm said.

"What would happen if we were caught at a checkpoint?"

"Depends who you are," Malcolm explained. "Normally, they'd just add ten years to the prison labor camp sentence of a sucker like me, profit from my slave labor and the 'upgrades' I shell out for most of the rest of my life. But since you're about to become a very wanted and hunted man, I imagine that they'd implicate me in your escape, and have me accompany you to that prison you told me about, for our 'ultimate rehabilitation.' Man, they got a way with language."

"I'm sorry," Winston said. "What will you do now?"

"I guess Clarita and I will move to Plan B."

"What was Plan A?" Winston asked.

An ear-splitting siren pierced the air, and the truck veered to another lane to let a police car whiz past. Winston braced himself against the wall to stop from sliding off his watermelon seat.

"Wait out two more years. Then move to the house we bought in Maroon Country, Jamaica, ten years ago. We used it as a vacation home for a few years until I got busted. Since then Clarita's rented it out for income. A beautiful place, up on a mountain."

"What's Plan B?"

"That's our shit-hits-the-fan plan. I escape from the prison plantation early, meaning my life's in danger. When they find out, Clarita's likely to be called in for questioning, too, maybe held hostage until I show up. So instead, she's tipped off in advance, calls in sick, packs a bag, grabs the cash, passwords for our offshore bank account, and jewelry, then flies to Canada. By the time they show up to question her, she'll be in Montreal, en route to Kingston."

"Did you manage to tip her off?"

"Yeah. I got word this was up yesterday, and called Clarita last night with our code words to make her move."

"Why didn't—"

"I couldn't tell you," Malcolm continued, "on the chance that our conversations could be bugged, or that you wouldn't want to go."

"I hope you make it. I hope we both do," Winston said.

"Damned right. But now it's a race against the clock. Our work crew supervisor will file a standard absentee report on us today, which just means you get assessed a big fine. It doesn't become a problem report until the second day. That's when they'll notice we're gone. By then, Clarita should be in a nice hotel in Canada, and we should be in Bed-Stuy, waiting for our one-way ticket out of the country."

Winston had heard stories of the Bed-Stuy ghetto, a lawless, walled-off mini-city of drug users, criminals, and the poorest of the poor, less than ten miles from his lower Fifth Avenue penthouse. He couldn't imagine hiding out there. "Why don't we just drive straight through to Canada right now?" he asked.

"This truck's not getting across that border. Neither are those drivers. Getting into the Bed-Stuy ghetto is a lot easier than getting out of the country."

"You ever been to the ghetto?"

"Back when it was just a few poor Brooklyn communities. Bedford Stuyvesant, Bensonhurst, East New York. But I've been on Tex's plantation since before the ghetto was closed off. We'll see it, probably in about twelve hours or so. Meanwhile, it wouldn't hurt us to get some sleep."

Winston handed him a sleeping bag and unrolled another one. The compartment was tight, but they managed to stretch out. The steady hum of the truck kept Winston up, but after a few hours he fell into a long sleep.

Malcolm was eating a chunk of melon when Winston woke the next morning. He handed a good-sized piece to Winston.

Winston ate as he stood and stretched in the tiny compartment. "You think we're going to get a bathroom break?" he asked, fairly desperate.

"That's what this is for," Malcolm grinned, holding out the hollowed out watermelon. "Seven traveling uses for a watermelon. Use number six: a lavatory." He flattened the bottom of the melon and propped it against a corner, then leaned a few other melons against it to hold it in place. "Use number seven: a lavatory holder."

Winston relieved himself in the hollowed-out half of the melon.

"How much further?" he asked, looking at his watch. It was about eight a.m.

"It depends on how far the George Washington Bridge security checkpoint is backed up. But we should be reaching there pretty soon."

"They've got all the latest scanning technology at the bridge. What if we're detected?"

"The Resistance has some pretty clever hackers working for it. A lot of kids who were blacklisted or kicked out of college, and even high school, for Homeland Security violations, or teenage drug offenses. They've made a life of this sort of thing."

"You mean our life depends upon a gang of sixteen-year-old

hackers with tattoos up the gazoo and pierced tongues?"

"Something like that," Malcolm smiled. "But don't underestimate them. There would be no Resistance movement without them."

"How's that?"

"The Resistance is organized into independent cells," Malcolm said. "The hackers manage the I.T., sharing open source code that allows them to hijack other people's computers and make them their untraceable computer server slaves. All coordination is done remotely, on the run, with pirate cyber drop boxes. I heard from newly arrived prisoners that this is how they keep ahead of the man."

"So the hackers run the Resistance?"

"Uh-uh. Each cell is divided into three functional areas: direct action, research, and information technology. They like to call them *DAREIT* gangs, as in: dare it and risk your freakin' life, cause it's all over if General Bashcrost's boys catch you."

"Why do they join the Resistance if it's so dangerous?"

"Why do any of us resist?"

"I've got no choice," Winston said.

"I bet that's how they feel."

The truck slowed to a stop. Winston pictured the Homeland Security sentry checkpoint at the George Washington Bridge, teeming with troopers and technology. For a long time, the only sound he heard was the truck, and vehicles around it, inching their way toward the bridge. Then, all at once, they heard two voices questioning Dawn, as a robot's electronic sensors were laid heavily on different parts of the truck.

There was a pause. Then the truck started again, picking up speed as it crossed the bridge into New York.

An hour and a half later, the truck slowed to a stop again for another checkpoint, this one at the entry gate of the sprawling Bed-Stuy ghetto. The inspection was quick. The truck continued loudly along a pothole-laden, rugged road through the busy streets.

"That one seemed easy," Winston remarked.

"Getting in is easy," Malcolm said. "The government views ghettos like Bed-Stuy as urban sewers, places to flush their drugs, criminals, free-thinkers, and lunatics. But it's getting out that can take half a day, waiting for identity checks and strip searches."

The truck slowed down, backed up, and pulled to a stop. Winston and Malcolm heard Dawn talking with a few people, then the sound of the back of the truck opening.

Winston heard a forklift approach the back, and workers unloading crates of watermelons, but he and Malcolm could see nothing from their hidden compartment.

From inside the truck, Quinn shouted, for their benefit, "This will do it for this market, Dawn. Let's keep moving. We'll unload the rest at the next stop."

The truck pulled out and drove a few more miles. It backed up again and came to a stop. Quinn moved crates and melons around, then slid open the entrance to the hidden compartment.

"C'mon out," he called. "We could use your help unloading."

They walked off the truck and found themselves parked in one of the three loading docks of a large food market in the center of the ghetto. After stretching their legs and using a toilet, Winston and Malcolm joined Dawn and Quinn in unloading the remaining half truck of melons onto pallets and carts. The produce manager of the store registered the shipment on his handheld and spoke with Dawn. Market employees moved the pallets into the store, and within fifteen minutes, they had unloaded all but a few dozen watermelons.

"These are for our camp and a soup kitchen," Dawn said. "Let's head over— "

Dawn stopped when she noticed an armored sports utility vehicle pull to a sudden stop right outside the loading dock. Two young Chinese men in the olive-green shirts and pants of paramilitary camouflage, wearing slick sunglasses and baseball caps, jumped out of the car and ran toward them. One carried an M-16 assault rifle, which he trained on Winston, Malcolm and Quinn while he moved quietly to the side. The other, wearing a thick gold gang chain and pointing a semi-automatic shotgun, quickly guessed that Dawn was the leader, and approached her.

"You didn't pay us to unload here," he said angrily.

"Why the fuck would I do that?" she stared at him coldly.

"'Cause everybody pays us. We work for Chang Yu."

"I'm supposed to know who the fuck that is?" Dawn snarled.

"You got a big fucken mouth," the gangster said, moving menacingly closer. "Why don't I make you suck some hot lead from this barrel?"

"Look, I got no money. You want a melon?" Dawn scooped up a large, round melon from the open back of the nearby truck. "You want it?"

"I don't want no fucken—"

"Here—take it!" She threw the melon at the gunman. He stepped aside to dodge it, and in that split-second, Dawn smashed out his knee with a savage kick. She spun forward, pushing the gangster's gun barrel down with one hand, then followed through with her other elbow, which landed like a hammer against his head.

As the gangster's partner turned and re-aimed his assault rifle, Dawn slid to the ground and picked up the fallen shotgun in one fluid motion, immediately squeezing off a thunderous blast, blowing the other thug off his feet.

"Quinn," Dawn snapped. "Get the rifle and frisk him. We could use the weapons. Any phones, too."

Quinn picked up the fallen rifle, frisked the badly wounded man, and removed a phone and an automatic pistol from an ankle holster.

The other gangster regained his senses and rose unsteadily on his battered knee. "Wu's not gonna let you—"

Dawn slammed the gun barrel against his head. Blood spurted from his mouth. "You still threatening me, scumbag?" She bent over, patted him down, and took a phone, a pistol, and bullet cartridges from around his belt. "Now get up, and drag what's left of your partner outta here."

The gangster slowly limped to his wounded partner. With great effort, he started dragging him out toward their car.

"You better fucken run," she shouted, aiming the shotgun at his head. "before I lose my fucken temper!" The gangster picked up his pace.

"Winston, Malcolm," Dawn yelled. "We gotta move, fast, before their friends get here. Get in the front seat with us."

Winston crammed into the front seat, followed by Malcolm and Quinn, who sat halfway out the window.

Dawn slid the handgun to the waist of her pants, laid the shotgun on the floor and jumped into the driver's seat. Winston's leg and arm pressed against hers as she started the truck and backed quickly out of the loading dock. Her sleeveless tee shirt was moist with sweat, and she took short, fast breaths. She wiped her forearm across her sweaty brow. Up close, Winston was impressed by her magnetism.

As she floored the gas and raced the truck down the street, Dawn half turned toward Winston, smiled, and swiftly licked her lips.

"Welcome to Bed-Stuy," she said.

NINETEEN

Dawn weaved the tractor-trailer through the crowded streets of the Bed-Stuy ghetto. Cars and trucks were parked, double-parked and parked sideways over curbs, obstructing the heavy traffic. The central lanes were populated mostly by old, dented vehicles, as well as bicycles, handcarts crammed with merchandise, and pedestrians.

People seemed to be everywhere in the Bed-Stuy ghetto, crowding the sidewalks, hanging out the windows of tenements, cramming into the slow-moving, overflowing vans that served as mass transit. Screaming children of every nationality played in doorways, panhandlers blocked crosswalks, preachers stood on stepladders, warning of hell and seeking converts.

Winston had expected to see vacant storefronts and boarded-up buildings. But nothing was vacant, no space went unused. Armed guards framed the doorways of many of the grocery stores, computer cafes, and ethnic restaurants, while pushcart vendors of every product imaginable peddled their wares along the crammed sidewalks.

"It feels like Calcutta," Winston said to Malcolm, who was squeezed into the front seat between him and Quinn.

"There's one of these in every large city in America," Dawn said. "Ours just happens to be the biggest."

"And the wildest," Quinn added enthusiastically.

"Operation Clean Sweep displaced millions of hard working folks from their jobs," Malcolm said. "Paid workers can't compete with free prison labor. Between that, the families left behind from those of us imprisoned, high unemployment to begin with, and fourteen years of what the Administration has been calling 'welfare reform,' about half our country now lives in places like this—or the place we just came from."

Every few blocks, Winston could see the armored Hummers and luxury cars of local drug dealers, whose street soldiers guarded busy open-air drug markets. He had read about the drug bazaars, which brazenly sold every illicit substance known, but was still amazed at how openly they functioned.

"Are drugs the biggest business in Bed-Stuy?" he asked.

"Seems like it," Dawn said, braking suddenly to avoid hitting a man being chased across the street by two other men carrying weapons. "Big Brother tries a lot harder to keep newspapers out of the community than crystal meth, smack, crack—or guns." As she resumed driving, they heard a series of gunshots.

Quinn picked up the pistol from the floor and set it on his lap for easier access. "Our revised Second Amendment at work. They encourage the gun peddlers and drug dealers. They'd rather have them running Bed-Stuy than the Resistance. Besides, half the dealers are undercover Homeland Security agents or bounty-hunting marshals."

Dawn slowed down and double-parked the truck, keeping the engine running. "Winston, you come with me," she said.

Winston followed Dawn to an open door under a banner that read, "Community Food Kitchen—All Welcome." A double line of hungry, desperate-looking people threaded its way down the street and around the corner.

Dawn told an older woman controlling traffic at the door that she had a delivery. The woman waved them in, and Winston followed Dawn into a large open dining room filled with long tables, benches, and hundreds of noisy people. People waited patiently in line as workers served food from behind a steel table at the far end of the room.

"Yo, Abie," Dawn yelled, then stuck two fingers into her mouth and let out a piercing whistle. An older man with a graying beard, long apron, and ornately-embroidered skullcap looked up from the serving area. He met Dawn at the side of the room with a big hug.

"You two come to volunteer?" he asked.

"Not today, rebbe," Dawn replied. "We got two dozen watermelons in the truck outside, though, fresh off the farm. Could you organize a few helpers with shopping carts? Nobody listens to me these days."

"Hah," Abe laughed, "everyone listens to you—even those that you may not appreciate." He nodded toward two hefty men with big shirts worn loose over their waists eating at a distant table.

"Don't worry," Dawn assured him, "we're not staying long."

Winston helped Dawn quickly unload half the remaining melons from the back of the truck into the arms of two helpers and their shopping carts. "A lot of churches and synagogues and mosques on the outside have presences in the ghettos," Dawn explained. "Their congregants work and live on the outside, then send their guilt money here. People would starve by the thousands without places like this and people like Abe. I respect what they do, but it's not my way. They deal with the symptoms, we fight the problem."

"Who gets more frustrated?" Winston asked, smiling.

"We both get frustrated," Dawn answered. "My kind just die a lot sooner."

They crowded back into the front seat of the truck. "Time to head home," Dawn declared, starting up the engine.

For the next forty minutes, they drove through the crowded streets. Winston stared out the window like a tourist visiting a foreign country for the first time. "How big is the ghetto?" he asked.

"It's bigger than most people think," Dawn said. "A quarter as long as Manhattan, and wider. But we're almost home."

"By tomorrow morning they'll know we're gone," Malcolm said. "They'll have your pictures from the prison camp's sentry gate. Me and Winston, they've got everything in their database except our smell. They'll be looking for us."

"That's why we're all about to disappear." Dawn pulled the truck to a stop. They had turned down a potholed side street that was littered with rusting and bullet-ridden cars. A thirty-foot-high corrugated steel fence nearby circled an entire city block. Quinn pulled a communicator out of his pocket, punched in a series of numbers and letters on the keypad. "Quinn, coming home," he said, holding it a few inches from his face.

"Optic and voice recognized and approved for entry," the communicator replied.

A gate in the middle of the fence whirred open. Dawn pulled the truck into a covered garage. The gate closed behind them as Dawn and Quinn opened their doors and climbed down. Winston and Malcolm followed.

Robotic sensor devices immediately began scanning the truck from the roof, walls and ground. Long muzzles in automated gun turrets followed their movements. Dawn led the others to a workshop area where they were met by two dreadlocked technicians in tee shirts and work boots, both young enough to still be in high school.

"We'll need to remove those prison bracelets, but first take off the patches we gave 'em," Quinn advised his two colleagues. "They worked great—fucken drones still think these dudes are in Florida."

"Sweet!" said the shorter of the two techies, a girl with shorter dreadlocks, sticking out her tongue and tapping the computer chip embedded in it against her teeth.

"Yo, but right now it's, like, not transmitting nothing," one of the kids with dreadlocks, a lanky boy, quickly observed.

"Du-uuuhh," Quinn replied, clicking his tongue-chip repeatedly against his teeth to make the point. "We're in a lead-coated black box garage. Nothing's transmitting in or out of here. So the prison computer just woke up to find itself scammed."

"You said the prison would know they were gone by this morning anyway," the other techie recalled.

"Right," Quinn explained. "That was our intel."

"Right on," the dreadlocked boy nodded, remembering the plan. "Scam the man, with, like, no fingerprints." He clicked his tongue-stud chip enthusiastically.

"You got it." Quinn pointed to a modified steel vise grip on the bench. "Winston, put your wrist in there, and we'll get it off."

Winston shuddered with the memory of the hand device that had been used to drug him at Kennedy Airport, but laid his wrist into the vise.

Quinn opened his communicator's three-dimensional keyboard on the work table and keyed in codes. Lasers activated in the vise grip and shot pinpoint beams over the bracelet.

"Cat," he said to the dreadlocked girl, without looking up. "Remove our patch . . . now. We want to save those smart little suckers."

"Sweet," she said, pulling the stamp-sized patch off Winston's titanium bracelet with tiny tongs.

The other young technician operated a small joystick with a built-in screen that he held in one hand. "Yo, like, whenever," he announced.

"On three, make the break," Quinn ordered. "One, two, three!"

The lasers whirred louder and blinding beams pulsed onto the bracelet from two sides. Winston looked away. In two seconds, he heard a loud clunk, and the lasers fell silent.

"Perfecto," Dawn observed. Winston's security bracelet had fallen neatly off in two pieces. "Booby traps disarmed. We loooooove you I.T.!" She turned to Malcolm, with a jubilant smile. "Next victim."

"Them bracelets are totally schwag," the girl named Cat commented to Malcolm as she laid his hand in the vise and carefully pulled off the patch. "Like, indestructible slave wear make-a-move-our-drone-will-fry-you. Fuck their prison camps and fuck their Party and fuck old man GOB!" She clicked her tongue-chip triumphantly.

Within seconds, Malcolm's bracelet was off.

"Thanks," Malcolm said to the young technologists, rubbing his liberated wrist. "That feels better. Eight years on a fucken prison plantation . . ." his voice trailed off as he shook his head in disbelief.

"We should arrange a dump drop to throw off their trail," Dawn proposed, pointing to the bracelet fragments.

"I see what you mean," Quinn considered it. "There's probably some transmission that takes place once the bracelet's broken. If we dropped the fragments somewhere else . . ." He handed her a small lead box.

Dawn turned and called to the dispatcher, who sat in a booth on the opposite side of the garage. "Mariko," she yelled, sweeping the bracelet fragments into the box. "I hear this truck's going to Cleveland today?"

Mariko stepped out of the booth. A squat, fifty-something Japanese woman, she looked into her communicator screen and replied, "Leaving in thirty-five minutes."

"We got a no-fingerprint dump to make."

Mariko took the box. "Where do you want them to leave it?"

"There's a rest stop on the Interstate, about twenty miles before the Cleveland ghetto. Garbage drop is fine. They'll think he's in Cleveland, waiting to cross into Canada."

"Also, Mariko, we've got a few dozen watermelons there to unload. Could you notify the café ? We gotta go in through the security booth."

"Got it. Fresh watermelon—yummy."

Dawn waved Malcolm and Winston to a small booth at the far end of the garage. "Bug and implant hazard check," Dawn explained with a shrug. "Community protocol. One at a time, after me."

Winston stepped into the booth next. In less than a minute, a voice announced he was clean and should exit through the door in front of him. He walked out to what at first seemed like a two-lane road carved through a junkyard. On both sides of the walk-way and along the perimeter, flattened cars were stacked thirty feet high until they nearly touched a series of enormous photo-voltaic tarps, which were duct-taped together to form a solar panel rooftop over the entire area. Powerful natural sun lamps were suspended from the roof, bathing the enclosed community in artificial daylight.

Dawn was waiting for him. "Is that a tank?" he asked her, looking straight ahead. A cannon and machine guns from an aging armored vehicle about a hundred feet away were aimed right at the security garage.

"It once was," she explained. "Engine's busted, but the guns work fine. We've got them rigged remotely, so nobody ever has to get into that thing."

Malcolm joined them from the security booth. "Pretty tight place you got here."

"It's probably safer in here than out there," Dawn said. "Hard to say. Hackers have kept drones out of Bed-Stuy for years, with a sort of electromagnetic disruptor field high above the whole ghetto. But that doesn't stop their undercover foot soldiers. Anyway, if they ever come to get us, it won't be pretty."

Malcolm and Winston walked with Dawn through the corridor, their eyes scanning the walls of flattened cars. Quinn emerged from the security booth and met up with the other young hackers.

"Could I get a message to my wife?" Malcolm asked Dawn.

"Will it be coded?" Dawn asked.

"We worked it out in advance," Malcolm explained. "I'll code it into her daily business news e-mail. She'll know what to look for."

Dawn nodded, impressed. "Quinn will take you to Info Tech's blue communication van. Make sure he enters first, and whatever you do, don't touch the doorknob until he opens it for you. Those kids love to rig shit."

"Thanks," said Malcolm, "and thanks for the ride out."

"For a man who was waiting out his sentence, you sure worked a lot on Plan B."

"Shit happens, so you go with it," Malcolm said, slowing down to wait for Quinn.

Winston and Dawn arrived in front of the tank cannon, were the corridor ended. To their right and left stretched what looked like a large parking lot for more than a hundred old trailers, buses and vans. Most had been decorated with artwork or political murals and customized with added levels on the roof. Music blared from a dozen different stereo systems, and a grungy rock band was practicing in the middle of the narrow road. Outcroppings of small tents, tables, armchairs and sofas formed tiny makeshift yards that overlapped one another.

Winston strolled through the camp alongside Dawn, watching half-undressed, wild-haired residents playing music, lounging around the circle, eating, smoking, talking. Most seemed much younger than he was. In his well-groomed, affluent world across the East River, he would have called them all misfits.

"Do you have to be under twenty-one to get in here?" he asked Dawn.

"We've got our share of gray-haired elders, too," she replied. "Wisdom doesn't fall from trees."

"Good thing," Winston observed. "I don't think anything would grow here."

"Actually, we got a kickass herb garden under lights by the east wall, medicinal herbs for community consumption and pleasure, as well as plenty of sprouts."

Dawn paused outside the customized shell of an ancient school bus. A skilled carpenter had extended the roof and replaced the steel sides with ornately carved logs. Winston could discern the figures of elves, dwarves, fairies, and a Noah's ark of animals in the carvings.

"Lemme guess," Winston said, impressed. "You're not only a getaway truck driver, martial arts warrior and irresistible Resistance leader, but you carved this rolling work of art?"

Dawn shook her head. "My father. And it hasn't rolled in years. He was a hippie carpenter. Used to take us around the country in this thing, to Rainbow Gatherings, fairs, campgrounds. He got drafted in 2009, shipped out to Pakistan right away. My mom and me each took three jobs to get enough money to buy his way out. But money's something we never had enough of. He was killed with three hundred other suckers in Karachi at the basic training camp."

"I'm sorry to hear that. Terrorists killed my dad, too, in the World Trade Center on September 11."

"That's terrible," Dawn said, growing angry. "I wish our government had just focused on those terrorists. We might have joined with the rest of the world and ended it right then. But I blame this Administration for my father's death."

"How's that?"

"Right after the Musharaf assassination, the American air force took out Pakistan's nuclear weapons, weeks before our first ground troops even arrived. These endless occupations have nothing to do with terrorism and everything to do with keeping this country in a constant state of war. Otherwise there would never have been a draft, and my father would never have been sent to Pakistan."

"You're right," Winston said, surprising himself. He had heard arguments like Dawn's during the first Iraq occupation, back in his college days, and had called them oversimplified. Now they seemed to make sense. "I wonder how many lives would have been saved had we voted against the Blush Administration's 'preemptive' war strategy back then?"

"When I was a little kid," Dawn recalled warmly, "my mother took me to those early antiwar demos, along First Avenue. But she was insane enough to keep protesting the wars, even after Patriot Act VI was passed. She became an early victim of the Homeland Security special prison system. We never even knew where she was sent for her 'ultimate rehabilitation.'"

"You . . . say your family used to take this bus to Rainbow Gatherings?" Winston asked softly, trying to change the subject. "I remember hearing about them when I was younger. What were they like?"

"They happened every year in a different national forest, in the week leading up to July 4th, ending up with a huge outdoor party celebrating independence. Before they fell victim to the war on our Constitution, my dad called them 'a gathering of the disparate elements of the American counter-culture.' I was young, but still had a great time while the party lasted."

Winston nodded at the encampment. "So is this what's left of the rainbow nation?"

"Not exactly," Dawn explained. "We're part of the rainbow nation, or maybe they're part of us now. It's all a matter of perspective, isn't it?" She carefully watched his reaction.

"What?" Winston said, feeling a bit uncomfortable.

"I'm always surprised when I'm with people who work for the other side. You seem sort of normal."

"What do you expect. Horns and red eyes?"

Dawn shuddered. "What goes on out there, the karmic consequence of their actions, it's just so . . . dark. And you've spent your whole life being part of it."

"I'm not dark," Winston replied defensively. "Just cynical. And, until recently, rich and happy and ignorant. But people change. Just provide them with a different . . . perspective."

Dawn grinned, almost shyly, looked into Winston's eyes, and turned to put her hand in a print reader that opened the van door.

"Dawn is home," she announced to her computer.

"Print and voice alarm deactivated," a soothing voice replied. "Welcome home."

Dawn turned in the doorway and waved Winston over. "Come on in."

The space was long and, despite its narrowness, cozy. The bus seats had been removed to make room for a long open living room and office, as well as a tiny kitchenette and bathroom at the end. A few comfortably worn armchairs, with their stuffing exposed, held small piles of papers, books, and foreign news magazines. Winston's eyes felt heavy, and he yawned before he could stop himself.

"I'm tired too," Dawn said. "We drove through the night. I'll show you where you'll be sleeping," Dawn led him up stairs to a cocoon-like loft built into the roof. It held a large old waterbed and a dresser. "This is where you'll be. I'll stay close by."

"This is your room?"

Dawn nodded, moving some clothes off the bed and flipping the bedding over so that it looked half made.

"Where will you stay?"

She shrugged. "This trailer isn't big, but there's plenty of floor space and mats."

"That's very . . . hospitable of you."

"I noticed you were getting a little excited during our crowded truck ride today?" Dawn offered, tilting her head slightly and arching an eyebrow.

"Uhhhh," Winston was unsure how to answer. He immediately became aware of the blood rushing to his crotch. "Maybe I was," he smiled unsteadily.

"How long have you been alone?" She moved a step closer, staring at him with seductive, deep hazel eyes.

"A long time . . ." he confessed. "Too long. But I have a girl-friend, and we were . . ."

"She's living in another world," Dawn whispered. "And tomorrow we may both be dead. You know what Janis Joplin said?"

"I can't say I do." Winston stroked her bare arm with his hand. His heart was racing. He realized she was right—he would never see Lilly again.

"Get it while you can," Dawn urged. She removed her tank top with one quick motion and moved her body up to touch his. Her small breasts pressed against his chest, and her nipples were dark and hard. "Get it while you can," she repeated, and suddenly, her mouth was on top of his, her tongue probing, her hand teasing his erection.

TWENTY

Winston woke to the sound of someone moving nearby. Drapes were pulled over the room's small windows. He had no idea whether it was day or night, or how long he had been sleeping, or even where he was. For a moment, he felt like he was in his old bedroom in Greenwich Village, until he realized that the bed he was sleeping in was much smaller than his bed at home.

Winston had been dreaming about running through a junkyard with a gang of young activists. There had been a fight, gunshots, a woman's sensuous body rolling across a bed, the very bed he was in.

Suddenly a shade was pulled open, and soft light poured into the room. A girl with long blonde hair and cat's-eye glasses rummaged through a dresser drawer, pulled off her tee shirt, and tossed it to a pile of clothing on the floor.

Those breasts look familiar, he thought.

"Relax, Winston. It's still me under here. You've been sleeping for fifteen hours."

"Dawn?" he asked, squinting.

"I went to the cafeteria to get my look changed. Nothing our resident artists like doing better. I got you these." She tossed a paper bag onto the bed and rustled through a drawer till she found the worn tank top she had been looking for. Winston noticed that the rings had been removed from her nostrils and eyebrows and set in her ears.

"You look different," Winston said, trying to decide whether he liked it. He recalled what a turn on she had been the day before, then realized that he was still naked.

"I don't need to make it easy for the bounty hunters. Those pictures they got at your prison gate were just made obsolete."

Winston looked in the bag. Old jeans, a shirt in good shape, socks, used high-tech sneakers, underwear and a few tee shirts.

"Put 'em on," she said, encouragingly. "They should pretty much fit. Unless you need your prison labor clothes, I'll throw them in the community barter bin."

"I'm enjoying the absence of clothes," Winston joked, grabbing her arm and pulling her into the bed. She slid from his grip like a cat, flipped backwards on the bed, and was on her feet before he could look up.

"Malcolm is leaving for Canada in a few hours," she said, all business. "He'd like to say goodbye."

"Malcolm is leaving?"

"Is there an echo in here?"

Winston wondered what was bothering her.

"Paul sent me a pirate e-mail," she said, still tense.

"A what?"

"It's how we get info from Paul and others in the International Resistance movement. It's how we got the request to rescue you. Takes a bit longer, but we know nobody can read it along the way, at least we think we know that."

"I'd like to call and thank him."

"Forget voice or video from here on in. That part of your life is over."

"Understood," Winston said uncomfortably. He sat at the edge of the bed and started dressing. "But if you could help me get out an encoded e-mail, I'd appreciate it. Call me old-fashioned, but I like to express my gratitude when somebody saves my life. And that extends to you, my newly-blonde savior." He pressed his hands to his heart and looked at her.

Dawn kept her distance. "We do what we do, long as we're alive to do it. But Paul's interested in more than helping you escape. And so am I."

"What do you mean?"

"You probably already heard from Professor Malcolm that each Resistance cell has a political research group, as well as direct action loonies like me, and I.T. hackers like Quinn and his rasta wannabee crew."

Winston nodded as he tried to figure out how the laces worked on the ultra-modern sneakers he had pulled out of the bag. "Malcolm did explain that little bit."

"That little bit is all most folks need to know, but your case calls for greater detail. What happens is that across the country, political research teams communicate with each other regularly, again through hijacked computers, sending encoded messages to offshore e-mail accounts that are picked up by other hijacked computers that each cell's I.T. team taps into. We even conduct virtual debates, bringing issues to every Resistance cell to discuss and vote on."

"Why are you telling me this?"

"I'll get to that, if you let me finish. You know the Resistance movement is new, and hasn't done much yet, but—"

"Stop right now if you're about to tell me about bombs or attacks you're planning," Winston said, annoyed.

"The Resistance has never engaged in terrorist violence and never will," Dawn said, folding her arms defensively. "There's enough of that coming from Washington and Al-Qaeda. What I was saying is that the Resistance councils have resolved that the only way we can convince our fellow Americans to rebel is by getting *our* message across on *their* mainstream media. Then—"

"Hah," Winston interrupted. "Talk about idealism interfering with rational thought. You got as much chance of doing that as I've got of getting my old job back."

Dawn shot him a scolding glare. "You gonna let me finish?"

He noted how quickly anger seethed through her, and made a mental note not to interrupt again. "Sorry."

"Our I.T. units also communicate with one another, hijacking computers continually and sharing code and know-how. The hacker kids have been working for more than a year on what they like to call Operation All Eyes Open. Without going into technical details, which I barely understand, it will allow us to hijack the computers responsible for the Homeland Security emergency satellite upload and use them to broadcast two or three hours of Resistance agitprop on their Channel Always-On."

"Wow!" Winston remarked. "You mean every household in God's United States will be force-fed your propaganda for two hours?"

"Maybe more, maybe less, depending on how quickly Homeland Security's Cyber Terrorism units can override the hijacking."

Winston thought about it a moment. Until two months ago, he had been making propaganda videos for the very federal agency that suppressed this sort of dissident information. "I still don't see why you're telling me this?"

Dawn paused and watched him closely. "Because the agitprop that we plan to simulcast is the BBC's *1984* movie, set in Washington D.C.—and you're the American who wrote it. Our political research team here in Bed-Stuy—it's one of the best in the country—they want to work with you on a preface, where you tell everyone why you wrote it, and what you witnessed at the killing prison. Nobody has ever lived to tell that tale before."

Winston shook his head in disbelief. "You're fucking with my head, you wild and sexy thing. C'mon."

"No shit," Dawn was dead serious. "The Resistance needs you, Winston."

"What are you talking about?" Agitated, Winston stood up in his new clothes, looked in the mirror, and didn't like what he saw. With his days-old stubble, unkempt hair, bleary eyes and hand-me-down clothes, he looked as though he hadn't had a respectable job in years. "Look, I don't know where you're going with this. Let's get downstairs. I need to say goodbye to Malcolm—and try to hitch a ride with him, unless being needed by the Resistance is the sort of honor that requires me to get chained down in this ghetto junkyard!"

Winston walked down the narrow stairs to the main level of the bus and headed toward the door. Dawn followed close behind.

"Don't open that door!" she said, in a domineering voice. "There's a security protocol for getting out as well as in."

"What is this place?" Winton demanded, whirling around to face her. "You've got to get through booby traps just to get out of your own home. I don't belong here!"

"Maybe you don't!" Dawn curled her hands into fists, and an ugly vein throbbed on the side of her neck. "You belong on Fifth Avenue in your fucken penthouse apartment, making propaganda videos justifying the systematic suppression and liquidation of people like my mother and, oh wait—you!"

"You know I can never go back," Winston countered. "But I can leave the country and find a new life somewhere . . . peaceful. What's wrong with that?"

Dawn stepped back and took a few deep breaths. "We risked our lives to bring you here to join us. But you're right—we can't force you to sign on. I thought . . . I thought maybe after yesterday you might want to. I guess I was wrong."

Winston moved closer and forced a smile. "This isn't about you. I'm not the rebel type. I could go anywhere from Canada, be part of a different country. But I don't see myself fighting against our way of life."

"Your way of life," Dawn corrected him. "Anyway, you try to leave the country now and they'll be looking for you. Wait a while, work with us for a few months. Let them think you're in Cleveland, where we dropped the prison bracelet. Take control of the timetable and you'll be more likely to escape."

"I'm sure they're looking for Malcolm, too. How is it that he's getting out?"

"We'll get Malcolm out through the black nationalist underground railroad," Dawn explained. "They're eager to get him to freedom and back to contributing to the voice of the Resistance again. He was an outspoken writer and professor once upon a time."

"How will he get to Canada?"

"There's an African-American church in Buffalo that's planning a bus tour of Niagara Falls tomorrow morning. They'll hide Malcolm tonight, and doctor the ID of a recently deceased man to get across the border at our end. The checkpoint out is easier than coming back in, where he would need a DNA match. But he won't be coming back in."

"I could do the same thing," Winston insisted.

"We don't have a sponsor to take you across yet," Dawn gritted her teeth and tried to control her temper.

"Well why the hell is that?" Winston demanded. "It's wrong that Malcolm ended up in that prison camp, and I'm glad he got out with me. But I thought yesterday's escape was about me, not Malcolm. So how is it the underground railroad is taking him, and I'm stuck here waiting for some bounty hunter to slice my fucken head off?"

"We can protect you," Dawn offered. "It's different in the ghetto. We keep the drones out, we have allies. We can fight them."

"Who said anything about fighting?" Winston demanded.

"When did I sign on for this fucken holy war? I just want to get out of this—I just want to survive."

"I want to survive, too. All of us do," she said. "Life is about survival, but not just about survival. Maybe we're also here to fulfill something."

"What would that be?"

"I don't know . . . maybe to experience our full potential?"

"What if I just pursued that experience from Canada? What's wrong with that?"

"You're not in Canada," Dawn said softly. She moved closer and pressed her face next to his. "You're right here. Right now."

Winston stared into her deep hazel eyes. She was beautiful, intoxicating. But he had known her for less than two days. She barely seemed to value her own life, he thought. How could he trust her with his?

"By tonight I could be in Buffalo," Winston said, stepping away. "And tomorrow, or the next day, Canada."

"Fight or flee," Dawn said, with a sudden urgency. "The choice is always yours, unless you're cornered, in which case, you have to fight. Or trapped, in which case, you have no choices."

"That was ultimate rehabilitation. No choices there . . ."

"Just despair, I imagine," Dawn said. "I've imagined it a thousand times."

Winston shuddered. "I never want to be there again."

"My mother was never given a second chance. You're lucky."

"We make our luck." Winston stared at the wall. The air was still. He listened to Dawn's quiet breath. "And we make our choices," Winston said finally. "I've been given a second chance. I choose to leave. I choose to live."

Twenty-one

Dawn walked quickly, staying two paces ahead of Winston as they marched to the community dining hall. Each time he tried to catch up, she quickened her pace, as though he had some sort of contagious disease. He finally gave up trying and followed silently, looking over the old vehicles that formed the Resistance camp.

Every battered van, bus or truck had been converted to reflect the style of its owner. Sword and sorcery, fantasy and heavy-metal motifs were popular, as were political murals and slogans.

Winston noticed that the only large space in the Resistance camp was the dining hall, a centrally located structure made from four gigantic shipping containers laid at right angles to form a large square. Some industrious welders had carved windows and skylights out of the steel containers, and artists had painted murals along the outer walls depicting the history of antiwar protest in America.

Dawn reached the dining hall entrance and slammed open the

door. Winston thought how ridiculous she looked as an angry blond. But it didn't matter anymore. Their fling the day before had been nothing more than two lonely people releasing pent-up sexual energy. Now they could get on with their lives. Winston wondered whether Lilly would be willing to move to Canada.

"I guess your first meal with us will be your last," Dawn said bitterly, as she entered the steel structure. "I'm so glad we were able to be of service."

"You're taking this too personally," Winston replied, smelling cooked food and feeling tremendously hungry. "It has nothing to do with you."

The cafeteria was half-filled with members of the Resistance community eating a leisurely breakfast. Dawn turned and put her face next to Winston's, trying to control her temper and not be overheard. "Shut up, just shut up!" she said angrily. "Look, Malcolm's in the courtyard out to the left," she pointed to an open door leading to a seating area. "Grab some food and tell him you're to be dropped off with him in the Buffalo ghetto. It's a small community, dangerous, and you'll be on your own. But maybe you'll be able to take care of yourself. You seem really good at that!"

"Where are you going? Can't you just sit with us and say goodbye?"

This only enraged her more. Then she breathed heavily and calmed down. Winston spied a tinge of regret in her seductive hazel eyes. He restrained an urge to pull her toward him for a farewell embrace.

"I'm going to walk around," Dawn said. "Hopefully when I return you'll be gone, and I can get on with our work."

Winston decided to let her have the last word. The witty responses that arose in his mind would only have made matters worse. Hadn't she been the one to initiate sex? He didn't recall making a commitment to staying with the Resistance as the nego-tiated price. It had just happened. Anyway, he was hungry. He needed to grab some food, find Malcolm, and move on.

A few dozen people sat at long common tables, while a kitchen staffer kept the self-service food counter stocked. The fare was basic: a big steel pot of oatmeal kept warm on a hotplate, nuts, dried fruit, whole wheat bread, jams and peanut butter, urns of coffee and tea and slices of the watermelons that they had trucked in from the prison camp.

Winston filled his tray with some of everything while he looked around for Malcolm. He didn't see him inside, so he took his tray and headed through an open door to the central courtyard.

The courtyard was a large internal square created by the steel containers. There were several small meetings taking place at picnic tables, and a large meeting area in the center of the yard, formed by dozens of beat-up armchairs and couches circling a small, ash-filled fire ring made of stone.

Simulated natural light beaming from the photovoltaic tarps on the roof of the compound gave the courtyard an outdoor feel. Winston spotted Malcolm and Quinn at a small table. He brought his tray over and sat down just as Quinn was leaving.

"So what's the word?" Winston asked, shoveling a large bite of food into his mouth before he had even sat down.

"Eat slowly or you'll choke," Malcolm advised. "Have you come to say goodbye?"

"Nope," Winston said, sipping some chicory bean coffee and wishing it were the real thing. "I'm supposed to ride with you through to Buffalo."

Malcolm seemed surprised. "Hmmm," he said, waiting for an explanation.

"It's not as though you're sticking around Bed-Stuy waiting for the bounty hunters to get you," Winston said, defensively.

"I don't have a project coming due—or a vivacious young lady wanting me to stay," Malcolm said

Winston wondered how much Malcolm knew.

"I'm planning to do my part from Jamaica," Malcolm continued. "I can't say I'm not disappointed in you, Winston. But I've been in the movement long enough to know that this here is an all-volunteer army, unlike the one we've got out there occupying other countries."

"Thanks. I'll take that as your approval." Winston smiled uneasily. He wondered what would happen in Buffalo after Malcolm left.

Malcolm filled him in on the escape plan out of the ghetto. The owner of a small fleet of refrigerated dairy trucks was working with the Resistance, and had allowed the I.T. unit to create a secret compartment with deeply embedded electronic masking devices. The truck was making deliveries in the ghetto, and then heading out to dairy farms in the north to make pick-ups.

"Why can't we just take the truck to Canada?" Winston asked.

"Trucks licensed to deliver to and from the ghettos are forbidden to leave the country," Malcolm explained. "Besides, there are complete physical inspections at the American border into Canada."

Malcolm checked his watch. "We've got to be by the main gate in twenty minutes. People wash their own dishes here. Opposite end of the square from where you came, then make a left."

Winston quickly finished what was on his plate and stood up.

Malcolm looked concerned. "I hear Buffalo's a small ghetto, and dangerous if you don't know anyone. You sure you're making the right decision?"

"It's close to Canada, and that's where I've got to get to," Winston said, feeling less confident than his words.

Winston brought his dishes inside and quickly washed everything at the washing station. As he started back to the courtyard, a tiny five-year-old girl with red hair rushed directly into his path. He stopped short so he wouldn't bump into her.

"Run away!" she shrieked, in the middle of a game.

"Why?" Winston asked, laughing.

"The troopers are coming, the troopers are coming! They'll kill us. Ruuuuuunnnnnnn!"

Right behind her was a robust woman of about forty, in an old pair of men's army boots, a steel serving bowl set as a makeshift helmet on her head. "Fi-fi-fo-fum, I smell a subversive Americun," the woman said, stomping her legs heavily as she chased the little redhead girl.

The child spun around, ran right up to the woman and, jabbing her finger in the air, yelled, "I'm in the Resistance and I can say whatever I want. We live in the ghetto and bad people can't come in here. I know the magic words. 'Know thee by thy works, know thee by thy works, know thee by thy works!' Hah-hah, I said it. Your lies don't work here and you can't boss us. Now you have to go back!"

"Ohhhww," howled the woman acting like the trooper. "Tara knows the magic words and I can't come into the ghetto."

The girl ran up to Winston again. "Hah-hah. See! I know the magic words."

"Thanks for making the trooper go away," Winston said.

"She's not a real trooper," the girl confided. "She's my mommy and her name is Mariah." Winston had a strange sense that there was something familiar about the girl.

"Mariah," Winston repeated the name slowly, trying to place where he had heard it. The air in the large room suddenly felt stale and hot. His mind pulled him back to the killing prison, and the Catholic activist in the cell next to his. "Tara . . . and Mariah . . . O'Neil?"

Mariah stopped short. "Tara," she instructed, "Go play with Alicia over there." Tara ran off. Mariah stared at Winston suspiciously. "I never forget a face. We've never met before. How do you know my name?"

"Brain talked about you. I was in the cell next to his."

"You were in the cell next to Brian," Mariah took a deep breath. "That would have been three months ago. But now you're here. And he . . ." Mariah's voice dried. She looked aside at her daughter, took another deep breath, pulled a water bottle from a bag and drank deeply.

Winston could suddenly hear the sounds of Brian's vicious murder as though it were happening all over again. He closed his eyes tight, opened them, looked at Tara, and felt a powerful urge to change the subject and never revisit it. "You . . . you have a courageous daughter," Winston said.

"Takes after her father," Mariah said proudly. "God rest his soul."

Tara ran back to them, wrapped an arm around her mother's thigh, and looked up at Winston. "I heard you say Brian. What did you say about my daddy?"

"What did I . . . what did I say?" Winston looked to Tara's mother for help. Instead, Mariah lifted the girl into her arms so that she could come face to face with Winston.

"Are you with the Resistance?" Tara asked, looking straight at Winston with piercingly bright blue eyes.

"No," Winston replied.

"Then why are you here?" Tara demanded.

"I was . . . I was rescued by the Resistance and brought here for my safety." Winston found the little girl's questions like a truth serum. He wished he could rush off, but he felt frozen in place.

"Did they rescue my daddy, too?"

"No . . . they didn't."

"Why didn't they rescue my daddy and bring him back here? He was in the Resistance and you're not."

"That's true. I don't know the answer to that."

"Did my daddy help you escape?" Winston felt as though her eyes were burning a hole through him.

"No. The nice people here in the camp helped me escape in a . . ." Winston stopped talking. His face grew pale and time seemed to stop. Suddenly he was back at the killing prison, trying to catch his laces onto the over-hanging pipe. Brian had called to him from the adjoining cell. "Isn't it too soon to give up hope?" he had asked.

"Wait," Winston corrected himself. "Your daddy did help me. When I wanted to take my own life. Your daddy gave me . . . hope, he gave me hope against fear. That's what he said, all the time, hope against fear."

"Is my daddy dead?" Tara shrieked, so loudly that everyone in the dining hall could hear her. All conversation stopped as Winston felt dozens of eyes on him.

Winston looked desperately at Mariah to let the girl down or take her away. Instead, Mariah said, "Please answer her question. She's been asking it for three months."

"Yes," Winston said grimly. "Your daddy is dead. He had hope against fear and love for you and your mommy until the very end."

"NOOOOO!" Tara wailed. "NOOOOOOO!"

Mariah cradled her daughter to her chest. Winston was unable to feel his legs as he drifted back to the courtyard. "What are you doing, brother?" Brian had asked. "What are you doing, brother?"

Winston sat on a bench, mumbling the words to himself, over and over. Brian's caring voice echoed in his mind, alongside the horrific sounds of his death.

Malcolm wandered over. "You okay?" he asked, putting an arm on Winston's shoulder.

"Hope against fear," Winston said.

"Listen," Malcolm said patiently. "We've got to get moving. Our ride leaves in just a few minutes."

Winston shook off the fog of his memories, and looked around. "I'm not going," he abruptly declared. The words surprised him, as though they came from a room that that he had entered for the first time. He thought of Brian's death, his courage, his fatherless daughter. He looked around him and felt a profound sense of gratitude for life. He knew what he had to do.

"You sure?" Malcolm asked.

Winston nodded. "It's time to fight," he said.

TWENTY-TWO

Winston found Dawn and returned with her to the small office in her bus. She was defensive, but eager to test the seriousness of his newly-proclaimed commitment to the Resistance. A coded e-mail from Paul Goode was waiting for him on her computer. The BBC's *1984* film was set to begin production the following week, and the producer was requesting script changes.

"How do I respond without bringing Homeland Security to your doorstep?" Winston asked, not wanting to touch the keyboard.

"Paul sends and receives coded communication through e-mail accounts he accesses in England, which we access stateside by hijacking computers outside of the ghetto to act as our slaves. Quinn and his gang have our untraceable network change slaves every hour, mostly corporate and office computers so that nobody gets into trouble. But they've also got a long list of favorite politicians and law enforcement types they like to tap into."

"It sounds like they have a good time."

"For orphans—which most of us in here are, if you hadn't guessed by now—we manage to have a pretty good time, at least as long as we're alive. You never know what happens next."

She smiled affectionately. Winston suddenly found himself appreciating her blond hair disguise and pulled her onto his lap for a short kiss.

This time Dawn didn't pull away. Minutes later, they were locked in a passionate embrace on the narrow, carpeted floor of the bus.

The weeks that followed found Winston working on the script every day, breaking only for meals and lusty, unscheduled bouts of lovemaking.

Dawn provided him with the tools and technical support he needed to work. She left him alone many days, for meetings, workouts and her periodic trips out to the ghetto for supplies. Winston never went, and worried about her each time until she returned.

On many evenings, Winston joined the late night music jams that the community held in its central courtyard. Drumming, dancing, and singing around their small fire all became inevitable when more than a few dozen of members of the Resistance community got together. Winston found himself looking forward to the frequent "celebrations of life."

By the end of his fifth week in the community, Winston had completed nearly all of the story line revisions the BBC had requested, as well as some that they hadn't asked for. He revised Big Brother's propaganda, to make it more compelling than in his original draft, and strengthened the movie's love scenes between the character Winston and his lover Julia. His powerful desire for Dawn helped make the changes convincing.

Dawn read everything, providing more timely feedback than the BBC, which only got messages, through Paul, back to Winston once a week. On a hot early August afternoon, as

Winston worked in his boxer shorts and nothing else, he asked Dawn to read through a difficult passage of his final edit.

She had just returned from a karate class she taught in the courtyard and was still wearing her white robe and black belt. Winston was having difficulty with the producer's request to modify the geopolitical alliances in the screenplay. Dawn read quietly, then set the script down.

"You're still not there," she said. "You need to make it more of a reflection of what's really happening today."

"I've been doing that," Winston replied, defensive and frustrated. He got up to refill his coffee and sank back down in the chair. "The BBC is calling it *1984/2014*, and setting it in a decrepit, post-industrial society. I've got to keep the sudden change in alliances intact, since it's important to—"

"I know," Dawn offered. "But why keep the same cast of superpowers as the old book? Why not use what we've got today?"

"That would only make it less believable. We've got a European Community bloc, a Chinese bloc, and America, the military superpower. But we're not even at war with any of those places."

"Right. But we are at war with a group of fundamentalist Islamic states, and the nature of our wars and alliances changes, just like Orwell wrote about." Dawn dropped a notepad in front of him and drew a set of circles and lines. "Give up on the book's three-state world, and this could work. See, Saudi Arabia was an ally, then the fundamentalist takeover made it an enemy, then America forced its way in and re-imposed a puppet state monarchy—friend again. Same country. Pakistan started as an ally, got armed by the old U.S.A., which backed the military dictatorship as long as it was pro-American, and then switched to an enemy days after Musharaf got assassinated by fundamentalists. See, the shifts happen overnight, and the state erases all record of the nature of the previous relationship."

"I get it!" Winston said enthusiastically. "And the biggest switcher of all—Osama bin Laden and Al-Qaeda."

"Exactly. Trained and armed by America to fight the Russians in Afghanistan, until big-time blowback leads to terrorist war against the west, the World Trade Center attacks, and everything since then."

"Great idea. I'll work with it," Winston said, typing furiously for a minute, then looking at her appreciatively. "You know, for one of the warrior class, you sure know a lot about politics."

"I was in a political research unit for a few years before I switched over to direct action. The Resistance makes you commit to one or the other, and I always did like action.

"Why?"

"I believe in fighting back. I figure someone's got to do it, since people like my parents aren't around any more."

Winston cupped her cool hand in his and held it to his chest. "We come from such different places," he said. "Thank you for helping me get here."

"Just doing my job," Dawn smiled.

"So what happens next, once I'm all done with this?" Winston asked. "It's going to feel funny waiting for the film to appear with no work to do. I like to have deadlines."

"I'm glad to hear that," Dawn smiled. "Now that you're about done with the first part, I was hoping we could get moving on part two."

"Part two? You mean the interview with me about the script? That won't take long."

"Not that," Dawn said, opening a drawer and pulling out a folder of papers. "I didn't want to distract you until you were finished with the revise. But our main strategy group, the virtual group of direct action cells all over, has been debating how to best capitalize on the *1984* simulcast."

Winston rubbed his hand along her body playfully. "And what new role did the Central Committee come up with for special agent Winston Smith?"

"We're running the simulcast, for as long as we can keep

Homeland Security's Cyber Terrorism goons from breaking it up. It's a pirated broadcast, so the BBC has no say on how we air it. That means we own the commercials."

"What commercials?"

"Aha," Dawn sat up playfully and held up a finger. "That's exactly what I was getting to."

They started work on the Resistance propaganda campaign the next day. First they held a breakfast meeting with Grit and Susan, who were the community's graphic arts experts. The two women were about Winston's age, trendy, and long-time lovers. Unlike most lesbian couples who had escaped God's United States for Canada or Europe, they were Brooklynites who decided to stay and resist. They had been responsible for Dawn's makeover, half the tattoos in the camp, and a children's art program. They did most of their work from the dining hall that also served as cafeteria, school and meeting place.

The meeting continued back at the designers' "shop," a decommissioned recreational vehicle that stood on the far side of the camp. "Welcome to Design Central," Grit said, as she entered the passwords and opened the narrow door.

Inside was one of the most beautiful spaces that Winston had ever seen. Murals stretched across the walls, giving way to small painted canvases with handmade frames. The furniture, mostly found objects from the street, was covered with fine colored cloth or painted in funky patterns.

Much of the space was given over to a studio area, which contained a modern computer design station, as well as a compact video production facility. "This is where we'll be working," Susan said, pulling over an extra chair.

"Where did you get all this?' Winston asked.

"Quinn's crew loves salvage jobs," Grit explained. "And Dawn . . . Dawn's a master of procurement."

"Don't ask, don't tell," Susan grinned.

Winston's collaboration in creating the content and slogans

for the Resistance's first ad campaign began with his desire to please Dawn. Within a few weeks, however, he realized that he was pleasing himself. Having spent years building ad campaigns that promoted the Blush Administration's radical right-wing agenda, he found himself eager—and adept—at refuting those very arguments.

He also found Grit and Susan able to produce every commercial that he could script. The I.T. unit helped them hack into any video or photo archive in the country, and the "Design Central" team were masters at image manipulation.

It was late October when Winston was ready to have the community see his first completed ad. Dawn arranged a screening in the dining hall, and nearly every member of the camp turned out. Winston realized how important the propaganda effort had become to the community. He felt a tinge of nervousness as the ad that he called *Two Sons* was tested.

"Two sons," the ad began, with a split screen simultaneously showing photos and then videos of George Blush and Osama bin Laden, from childhood to adulthood. "Both started out as the black sheep of their families, both became religious fundamentalists. Both lead their followers, in violation of the world community and international law, on a campaign of unending holy war. Both believe that the righteousness of their cause justifies the killing of millions of civilians, and both believe themselves to be answerable only to God and not the leaders of their chosen religions. One is an Islamic fundamentalist on a jihad. The other is the Christian President of God's United States."

The two screens converged into one of an American woman holding a baby in her arms and saying, in a perplexed tone, "But I thought we were the good guys." The image gave way to words that filled the screen: "SUPPORT OUR TROOPS—BRING THEM HOME!"

There was a short silence, then applause. Winston and Dawn took feedback from the audience. He felt a sense of satisfaction that he had never felt before. He was not just doing well for himself, or his boss, or even his Party. During his professional career he had always somehow felt like a huckster, like the messages he created were designed to mislead those who, according to his superiors, required misleading for their own good. The money had been extraordinary, as had the prestige. But something had been missing. He had always sensed it in the back of his mind, but had never been able to put his finger on it. Now there it was, all around him.

During the next five weeks, Winston felt creativity flow through him like never before. He built four very short commercials contrasting the Ministry of Truth's propaganda with facts, each ending with the slogan *"Whose truth?"* He scripted one ad after the next, taking feedback at weekly screenings, and revising them until they clicked. He had no idea if there would ever be the time or technology to air them, but that didn't matter to him anymore. When the time came, Winston's work would be ready. Fate, he realized, would decide what became of it.

TWENTY-THREE

A t seven in the morning on December 20, 2014, a Saturday, the BBC remake of *1984* was simulcast by pirated satellite transmission across God's United States on Homeland Security's Always-On channel. As required by law, more than two hundred million Americans trudged out of bed and watched what they assumed was an emergency government message.

Homeland Security's Cyber Terrorism division was caught entirely by surprise. Thousands of agents were mobilized, but it was more than three hours before they could wrest control of their satellite upload system from the well-coordinated teams of Resistance hackers that had hijacked it.

By that time, both the two-hour *1984* remake set in contemporary Washington D.C. and Winston's anti-government ads had been simulcast. There had even been time for Winston's scathingly critical fifteen-minute interview as the screenwriter of the movie. The interview had been conducted in advance through remote video hook-up with the BBC World Service. Winston had described his arrest for collaborating on the *1984* script, his kangaroo trial without an attorney, the sadistic executions he witnessed at the Homeland Security special prison, and the cronyism that marked the administration of what had effectively become, he said, slave labor camps. He presented data from Amnesty International showing that America's privatized prison population exceeded twenty million, with an estimated thirty thousand or more Americans executed per year, with no due process, under Homeland Security's policy of "ultimate rehabilitation."

After the interview, the Resistance aired more of Winston's "alternative public service ads," with dozens of gruesome images of dead civilians from American attacks in territories it had occupied across the Islamic world. The ads also provided country-by-country estimates from the International Court of Justice in The Hague of the number of civilian casualties caused by America's occupations. They added up to more than four million dead, and twice that number maimed or wounded.

During the four years since Patriot Act VI had effectively outlawed all broadcast media in God's United States except that created by Foxy News, the public had never even seen the casket of a single one of the hundreds of thousands of American soldiers who had died in the ongoing international wars against Islamic countries.

By the end of the third hour, the most subversive portion of the simulcast began, a ten-minute tutorial called *Everyday Resistance*. It opened with a concerned citizen asking, "This Administration is destroying our country, but they'll throw me in a prison camp if I protest. What can I do?"

An effort to incorporate ideas from Resistance cells around the country, this segment had taken the longest for Winston and Dawn to produce. For the final version, they boiled it down to the "Top Ten Tips for Everyday Resistance," beginning with "Take a vacation with the whole family out of the country, access the BridgeAmerica.can website for amnesty information when you get there, and don't come back until we replace this Administration," and "Volunteer to work in a ghetto community for a week—you never know who you might meet." Then came a "Small graffiti, big message" campaign encouraging citizens to write "We Want Our Rights Back," or simply "WORB," whenever they found a spot without a surveillance camera.

The American public watched one Resistance ad after another, unwilling to walk away from their screens because Patriot Act VI provided mandatory prison sentences for anyone violating Homeland Security's "must view" regulation. The Act also required that all television sets and video monitors be "Homeland Security-compatible," meaning that even many of the one hundred and twenty million poorer Americans living in urban ghettos "off the grid" found themselves watching the simulcasts.

To a nation accustomed to being fed carefully controlled propaganda for years, the effect produced was a combination of anger and confusion. The anger, for many, was first directed against whatever disruptive group was behind rousing them from their Saturday morning sleep. This soon turned to confusion about the accusations raised by the simulcast. For many millions of Americans, by the time the third hour was through, confusion had morphed back into silent anger, this time toward an Administration that had altered the very foundation of their democracy, an omni-powerful government that, for the first time, had lost all ability to regulate its airwaves.

Parents were at a loss for words when their children demanded explanations. Few decided to risk violating strict Patriot Act VI laws governing "subversive home speech." As mandated by law, parents informed their children that politics could only be discussed in school, and got on with their day's activities.

During Monday morning's mandatory simulcast of School News, a government spokesman described the "diabolical terrorist plot to weaken America by sabotaging our patriotic media with subversive rubbish."

Media Corp, the parent company of School News, Foxy News, and hundreds of other media subsidiaries, did not wait until Monday morning to assist the Administration. Less than an hour after Homeland Security had regained control of its satellite uploads, Foxy News began airing a star-studded twelve-hour news special titled *America's Media Held Hostage*.

America's Media Held Hostage pre-empted all programming on Foxy's nine news channels and Media Corp's other sixty-four cable and satellite channels. Both Secretary of State Bob O'Manley and Minister of Truth Russ Limetoff appeared together as co-hosts for the first time since Operation Traitor Recall.

Bob O'Manley began the special program with a moment of "silent Christian prayer," then introduced "this heinous act," as "the last desperate gasp of a dying far-left-wing conspiracy."

Attorney General John Bashcrost was on hand to sternly warn Americans that "anyone who heeds this treasonous call for illegal subversive revolution will be treated by our federal law enforcement army as no different than enemy terrorists."

Winston and Dawn watched the program from a video monitor mounted on the wall near her bed. They had popped open a bottle of champagne as their simulcast completed its third hour, then fallen into passionate celebratory lovemaking. They lay in one another's arms, sipping what was left of the champagne, gleefully heckling the famous pundits who appeared on the TV screen.

Secretary of State O'Manley asked his special guest the first question. "Now, can we assume, General, that when it comes to the capture and questioning of those behind this act of treason in Time of War, Homeland Security will be free to function under the Doctrine of Necessity?"

"That's correct," Bashcrost replied severely. "These conspirators might well know where the next biological bomb is hidden, and it is our responsibility, first and foremost, to protect ordinary Americans, their next victims."

"We've all been victimized by this already," Russ Limetoff

added. "I mean, we trust our media, and now this. Violation is a word that comes to mind, even rape. General, please tell us, especially those of us so outraged by this despicable act of cowardice—to hijack an emergency security channel to broadcast such hate speech against our government, please tell us—what can we ordinary Americans, what can the vast majority of us who are Patriotic Citizens, what can we do to help you protect us?"

General Bashcrost held up a small poster that the TV camera zoomed in on. Under large letters that said *"$5 MILLION REWARD, WANTED DEAD OR ALIVE, WINSTON SMITH,"* was a recent prison photo of Winston.

Dawn jumped up in the bed, spilling champagne all over the sheets. "Holy shit!" she yelled. "We've got to get you out of here."

Winston could barely believe what he was seeing. "What happened to the plastic surgeon that was supposed to come last week?"

"He's coming Monday morning," Dawn said, grabbing clothes and dressing quickly. "He's a volunteer doctor from outside the ghetto, but had to postpone last week, when I had planned it. We'll make our move Monday, right after he's done making you a handsome new face."

"The bounty hunters will be all over this," Winston said, his heart pounding.

"They don't know where you are. Just stay in the bus till Monday. I'll bring you food, and have Grit visit and give you a new hairstyle and colored contacts. Other than that, nobody comes in. I'll double-code the door, so stay put."

"Where are you going?" Winston asked anxiously.

"I'll find Grit, and make sure the camp is in high alert. We'll need to switch the front gate sentry to remote monitoring, stuff like that. I can't trust the coded phones right now. They'll be trying to flush us out."

"That might not be too hard," Winston said, panicked. "How can we get out of the country with a five million dollar bounty on my fucken head?"

"Plastic surgery Monday morning. After that, I have a plan. Trust me."

Dawn spread the alert through the camp and returned to the bus with Grit in less than an hour to begin Winston's makeover.

Despite the alarm, the other members of the Bed-Stuy Resistance community were eager to celebrate their victory. Their first battle for the hearts and minds of their fellow Americans could not have been more successful.

The techies from the I.T. group were especially proud of their achievement—the longest satellite transmission hijacking in history. They celebrated with a raucous, impromptu live music fest that stretched all day. Then Quinn and Cat took a drive out to another section of the ghetto, where they would party all night long at a big Saturday night Christmas rave.

It was past five o'clock the next morning when Quinn pulled the community cargo van into the security garage. The gate closed behind them with a clang, waking Cat, who had dozed off during the drive back from the party. Lori, a young woman in Goth-style black everything, sat between them, her duffle bag on the floor between her legs. Quinn had met her at a rave a few months earlier. This time he had managed to talk her into coming home with him, and he drove quickly, hoping she wouldn't change her mind. Given the community's heightened state of alert, Cat had agreed to keep his unofficial visitor a secret.

"We home?" Cat asked, yawning.

"Security booth, then straight to bed for you," Quinn replied, as he stepped out of the truck and walked to the entry booth with the others. He was still feeling the Ecstasy he had taken shortly after midnight, and had no interest in sleeping.

"Straight to somewhere else for you and me," Quinn said mischievously to Lori, who stood in front of him as they waited for Cat to be cleared through the entry booth. Quinn slid his hands over Lori's exposed belly from behind her, and nibbled on the back of her ear. She giggled and stroked his hand encouragingly.

"Meet you inside," she said, stepping in as the security booth door opened. It slid shut behind her as the sensors scanned her from all sides.

"Hey," Quinn noticed, yelling after her just as the doors shut. "You left your bag in the van." Quinn realized that she couldn't hear him from inside the booth. He walked back to the van, swung open the door, and grabbed the strap of Lori's duffle bag just as it detonated.

The explosion blew the van and countless shreds of Quinn's body high in the air. The bomb in the bag blasted open the fortified walls and ceiling of the security garage, sending flames a hundred feet in every direction.

Lori had just made it through the entry booth and begun running away from it when the bomb went off. She felt the scorching heat on her back and rushed to her meeting point to await the Homeland Security assault team.

Twenty-four

The bomb obliterated the Resistance camp's entrance garage. Because the sentry monitoring the community's front gate was in a van far from the entrance, she was unharmed. The sentry switched monitor cameras from the garage to the nearby street, to assess the size of the attack force. More than two dozen vehicles massed outside.

The sentry realized that the best she could do was to buy the community a few extra minutes. She punched in the emergency codes for an all-escape alarm, set the computer to track and fire at the approaching vehicles from the remote-controlled tank cannon, then grabbed her emergency kit and ran.

A shell scored a direct hit on the first Homeland Security tank arriving in the entrance, blowing it open before it could roll into position. The second tank fired back as it withdrew to the road. A body-armored trooper leaned out of a Hummer and fired an anti-tank missile into the compound.

Dawn roused Winston seconds after the first blast hit. She

threw on her clothes, grabbed her emergency kit and tossed him his. "We've got maybe six to eight minutes lead time, depending on our luck," she advised. "Get your clothes and keep quiet once we leave here. It's you they're looking for, and they'll be scanning for your voice once they destroy our defenses and the explosions die down."

Winston's heart raced. He threw his clothes on and pulled things from the emergency bag. Following her lead, he strapped a utility belt to his waist, set in a commando knife, portable light, mace, bullet cartridges and a 9-millimeter pistol.

Dawn spoke coolly, in a hushed tone, as though the danger were miles away, while she prepared her belt and dropped her communicator and a handful of important data chips into her escape bag. "Our robots should hold them off long enough for us to get to the tunnels. You don't fight Homeland Security head-on if you've got a choice, and we've designed this place so we'd have a choice."

She helped him strap on his night vision goggles and mini-headlight, and adjusted the bag around his back. "Let's move," she said. "Follow close."

"Wait," Winston touched her face. "Anything could happen out there. I want you to know. I love you."

"I was hoping you'd say that," Dawn pressed her lips urgently against his, and then pulled away. She punched in a code on the alarm near the door to make the bus self-destruct and led him stealthily into the night.

The air was putrid with black smoke. Missiles and bullets exploded around the entry road a hundred yards away. Dawn's escape hatch, a narrow tunnel, lay a few yards from the back of her bus, and they reached it in seconds. As they squeezed in, Dawn set a security code from her communicator, and Winston realized that she had also booby-trapped her tunnel entrance.

The passage was just wide enough for them to crawl through. After ten minutes, it opened up into an abandoned subway tunnel.

Winston stretched out his crouched body and looked around.

With the night vision goggles, he could vaguely make out the forms of escaping members of the Resistance community, running ahead of them. A couple of others arrived through another tunnel behind them.

He followed Dawn along the filthy subway tracks. Two enormous explosions behind them shook the ground, and then everything was still. Dawn flicked on a tiny amber light, looked at a hand-sketched map she pulled from her bag, then started down the tracks again.

The tracks were wet and slimy. Winston's boots were quickly soaked, but he did his best to keep up with Dawn, who marched silently for more than a mile. Finally she held out her arm for him to stop, and pointed to a steel ladder built into the concrete wall.

She was up a dozen rungs to the top of the ladder before Winston could start up behind her. But though she pushed hard at a thick steel grate, it wouldn't budge.

Winston arrived next to her and tried to help her push, but the grate was locked shut from the outside. Dawn pulled a tiny blowtorch from her bag, and went to work on the hinges. In four minutes, with both of them heaving, the grate finally opened up enough for them to wedge their bodies out. They found themselves near the curb of a quiet dead-end street.

A tough voice yelled, "Look what the sewers washed in, yo," startling Winston. A large, heavily tattooed man in a dark ski cap pointed an Uzi submachine gun at Winston's face. Winston raised his hands as the man disarmed him and stuck Winston's gun into his waist.

Another man pointing an assault rifle appeared next to Dawn, sizing her up appreciatively. His enormous arms burst out of a tight muscle tee shirt, and he wore a holstered sidearm. "Yo, Blondie, you light up Fat Man's territory with that torch of yours. Fat Man's crew owns you now." He licked his lips. "I don't know where you two are coming from, but I got some good idea about where you're going." The muscle man pointed the rifle at her with one hand, grabbed her pistol out of its holster with the other and rubbed it against his crotch.

"I spotted them first," the tattooed man in the hat complained. "I should get dibs."

"Whack the dude first," demanded a third man, who stood back in the shadows of the dim streetlight smoking a cigarette lazily, a shotgun leaning against his shoulder. "That way we all get a turn with the blond bitch."

"Lie face down, faggot, so I can get a clean head shot without splatting your brains all over my shirt."

Winston trembled. "Can't we . . . talk about this?" he pleaded.

The tattooed man smacked Winston across his head with the side of his gun. Winston fell to the sidewalk and struggled painfully to his knees.

"I said lay the fuck down, pussy-shit . . . Yo, Snake, this dude looks like someone . . . I know—I know—those bounty hunters were looking for him, different hair, but I swear it's the one in the poster a couple of the government boys showed me. They said there's a big reward out, big money, like five million."

"That's real money, Chigger," the muscle man replied, thinking hard. "That's fucked-up money."

"Fucken right five million is real money," the tattooed man called Chigger agreed. "And the government always pays what they promise when it comes to bounties."

"Those bounty hunters say whether he needs to be alive?" Snake asked.

"I don't remember, boss. Probably don't matter."

"I don't lose five million on probably don't matter. You got cuffs, Chigger? We'll cuff him, then fuck his whore real good, then bring him in for the money."

"Yo Snake, I saw him first, right?"

"Fuck that, Chigger. I'm the motherfucken lieutenant of this crew. Now did you remember the cuffs?"

"No, I didn't remember the fucken cuffs. What am I, your

pussy bitch? Yo, Porter, you remember the cuffs?"

"Shit, don't be looking to me for the cuffs," the third man said, flicking his cigarette butt aside. "No one told me about no cuffs."

"How many times have I got to tell you to be carrying the cuffs when you're with the crew?" Snake demanded.

"How many times I gotta tell you that I ain't your pussy bitch!" Chigger yelled back.

Snake suddenly swung his assault rifle toward Chigger and released a long volley of bullets. Chigger's body exploded in a dozen bloody fountains.

"How many times I gotta tell you not to talk back to me, motherfucker," Snake screamed at the bloody corpse. He turned his rifle to the third man. "You got something to say?"

Porter shook his head, nonplussed. "You the lieutenant," he said.

Before Snake had a chance to turn back to Dawn, Winston sprang from the ground and slammed full force into Snake's legs. As the big man toppled over, Dawn leapt straight toward his neck. She twisted his head between her hands and pushed with all her might. Snake's neck broke with a loud crack.

Dawn pulled Snake's lifeless body over her just as Porter started firing his shotgun. The pellets ripped into the corpse, splashing blood all over Dawn's shoulders. She pulled the automatic pistol out of Snake's holster, and pressed the trigger hard for rapid fire, releasing a fourteen bullet clip in Porter's direction. He dropped slowly onto the street, dead.

Winston's head throbbed where the gun had struck him. He rushed to Dawn's side. "You hit?" he asked. Snake's body was slippery with blood as Winston tried to pull it from on top of Dawn. It took three tries before he could get a good grip.

"I'm okay," Dawn stood up and seemed relieved that the blood drenching her shoulders and arms was not her own. "Take the Uzi. And check his pockets for cash. This Fat Man is a big-time dealer, so one of them is probably carrying a lot of it. We'll need it for later." Dawn rifled through Snake's blood-drenched cargo pockets and came out with a rubber-banded wad of hundred and thousand dollar bills four inches thick. She scooped up the assault rifle and put the pistol in her bag.

Winston took the Uzi from the ground where Chigger had been shot, but froze when he approached the fallen body. "Never mind, I got enough," Dawn said in a kind voice, and touched his hand softly. Winston noticed that her hand was trembling.

"We've gotta move fast," Dawn warned, pulling a mask from her bag and unpeeling it over her head. "Homeland Security will have detected the gunfire. There's a mask in your bag—put it on and follow me. The Fat Man's got eyes all over this neighborhood, and we don't want him to know who did this. Besides, this reward is going to complicate things."

Winston found a ski mask in his bag, pulled it over his face, and followed Dawn as she sprinted down the street, balancing the assault rifle in her arms as though it were a baby.

TWENTY-FIVE

Sirens wailed in the distance. As he sprinted down the sidewalk trying to keep up with Dawn, Winston realized that he had not heard a single siren during his six months in the ghetto. Now they were coming from a half-dozen locations at once. The Homeland Security Army's raid on their Bed-Stuy Resistance camp was being handled as a high-profile military assault.

It was six in the morning, dark and cool. Still, Winston was sweating and his breath was heaving as he tried to maintain Dawn's pace. He had started working out with her after his first week at the Resistance camp, and had been getting back into shape, but long distance sprinting was not something he had ever trained for. They had been running for at least a half hour, he thought, and must have covered nearly five miles. He trusted that she knew where they were going, but he also realized that she was taking them on a roundabout route along the edges of the gigantic ghetto, to avoid being spotted.

For the past ten minutes, he had been weighing the prospect of yelling for Dawn to slow down. His heart felt as though it were about to burst, and his throat was parched. His pride had kept his tongue in check, but he could not keep up with her any longer, and if she got too far ahead of him, he'd be lost, with hundreds of heavily armed troopers, bounty hunters and gangsters looking to collect the enormous reward on his head. He pictured his body with "$5,000,000" tattooed in a circular target across his chest.

Dawn's pace slackened just as Winston had resolved to shout for a rest. She walked a bit as he caught up with her. "We're nearly there," she said, also breathing heavily.

Winston collapsed against a nearby car, laying his torso over the hood. He waited for his breath to slow as he rummaged through his bag for a water bottle. Dawn drank from hers.

"We're gonna walk from here," Dawn advised, kicking the rifle she had been carrying under a parked car, then rolling the ski mask off her face and forming it into a hat. Winston pulled his off and slurped up half a liter of water before coming up for air.

"Put that back on when you're rested," Dawn advised. "You've become a very public figure. But we still have to get to Abe's kitchen, which, unfortunately, is in a busy area, even on a Sunday morning. You tired?"

"Just a little," Winston lied. "But I'm ready to walk."

They walked quietly for a few blocks, keeping their heads down as they passed a few early risers. Dawn stopped near a run-down tenement building, put a finger to her lips, and pointed upward. "Follow me," she whispered. "Stay close."

With pleasure, Winston thought to himself. He had to admit that he found her action mode appealing, with the sweat and sinews and heavy breathing.

"Clasp your hands like this, right here," she said, hunching slightly and interlocking her hands. Winston moved to the side of the building and did as instructed. Dawn stepped up into his hands and jumped to the side of the building, then bounced off it twelve feet into the air, her arms outstretched. Her hands grabbed the bottom rung of a fire escape ladder, which rolled down halfway to the ground as she dangled from it.

As Dawn ascended to the first landing of the fire escape, Winston jumped, grabbed the lowered ladder, and climbed up behind her. She pulled the ladder back to the landing and pointed upward.

They climbed the fire escape to the roof of the six-story tenement. Winston did his best to match Dawn's cat-like stealth as she glided past the steel-gated windows of the sleeping apartment dwellers. But he felt clumsy and loud, and was glad when they reached the roof.

There were very few tall buildings in the Bed-Stuy ghetto, so they had an open view of hundreds of decaying tenements. As he looked west, he could see the towers of Manhattan's skyline. It seemed far off and remote to him now, a modern, police-controlled island in a sea of deprivation and despair. Dawn tapped his shoulder and pointed in the direction they needed to head, then took off.

Although the rooftop stairwell entrances into buildings were heavily barricaded against entry, the buildings themselves were not fenced off from one another. Winston followed Dawn from one roof to another, slowing to jump down or climb up when the height of one building differed from the one adjoining it. They crossed diagonally over a large block of buildings this way, until Dawn stopped near the center of a five-story tenement, and made a signal for him to take some water and rest. She sipped from her water bottle and looked down from the edge of the building to the busy street, then nodded approvingly.

Dawn pulled a strong thin climbing rope from the bottom of her bag. She tied a slipknot around a ventilation fan attached to the roof, then tossed the long rope down the wide airshaft between the tenements into the tiny asphalt courtyard below.

She waved for Winston. By the time he had taken a good grip

on the rope and started down, she had slithered to the bottom and was waiting for him.

Winston joined her on the filthy landing of the courtyard. Dawn scratched lightly, but persistently, on a window, through which Winston could see a large dining room.

A middle-aged man in a small embroidered cap unlocked a heavy steel door next to the window and stepped into the dark courtyard. Winston recognized him as Abe, the manager of the soup kitchen where they had delivered the watermelons when he first arrived. Abe welcomed Dawn with a hug and looked at their rope.

"I take it this is the rainy day you warned me about?" His tone was grave.

Dawn nodded. "Can you open the clothing room in the basement for us?" she asked.

"I figured you would be around when I saw the simulcast yesterday," Abe said, leading them down a set of creaky stairs into the dilapidated storage basement of the soup kitchen. "Everybody's talking about it. Amazing work. But he better keep that hat over his face. I've never seen so many undercover marshals and bounty hunters handing out 'Wanted' posters. Highest reward I've ever seen, too. People take notice when there's a number that big. We tried to stop them from handing them out here. Like trying to hold back the ocean."

Abe opened the padlock of a gated area. Inside were shelves of old shoes and clothes, musty and rumpled.

"I've got to get breakfast started. We can feed your friend in the courtyard after you get what you left here." Abe rushed back up the stairs.

Winston worried about Abe turning him in for the reward. Dawn moved knowingly to the back of the gated area, where unsorted black garbage bags filled with recent donations were stacked ten feet high.

"Got it!" she said, grabbing a heavy plastic garbage bag stuffed full, with "For Julia" scrawled over it on a wide piece of masking tape.

"Who's Julia?" Winston asked.

"I'm Julia," Dawn said, with a mischievous grin. "In *1984*, she never got to escape. In the book, there's no struggle, not even a punch thrown. Big Brother's goons storm in, trap Julia and Winston, and it's all over—the end of their pathetic resistance. In our story, Julia gets away. And she rescues him so that he can be her reward."

"I've never been someone's reward before," Winston laughed, feeling flattered. He was amazed she could be making light of their predicament. But she had a plan.

"Take my small bag across your chest," Dawn said, tossing him her bag. She sliced open the garbage bag and pulled out an enormous fully packed army duffel. "We never would have made it this far if we'd had to drag this from my bus. I'll bring the bag to the roof. We'll put on our disguises later."

Dawn stuck her arms through the duffel straps and hiked up the stairs. Winston strapped her backpack to his front and headed up behind her.

"I hope we have time for coffee and a bite," he suggested from the stairway, as she emerged into the open room and set the heavy bag down on the long steel serving table.

Dawn noticed two husky men forcing their way into the door. The stocky woman with white hair who volunteered for front-door duty was blocking them. The men spotted Dawn standing next to Abe.

"Breakfast isn't until seven," the woman at the door said, holding her arms up. "Now you two just line up outside behind—"

Machine gun pistols suddenly pumped a deadly burst of lead from one of the man's hands, blasting the white-haired woman to pieces. Dawn dropped her bag and dove behind the steel table, knocking Abe to the ground beside her.

Winston stepped from the stairway into a hail of bullets.

TWENTY-SIX

Winston instinctively jerked back into the stairway just as an exploding dum-dum bullet tore up the doorframe.

Dawn pulled a concussion grenade from her belt and tossed it on the ground near the two bounty hunters just as they were fanning out. It exploded with a deafening *WHUNK* in the front of the room. The walls trembled. The gunmen and the volunteers near them were knocked unconscious.

"Winston, to the rope, move, now!" Dawn ordered. "Homeland Security will pick up the sound of the grenade and be here soon." Winston darted from the stairway through the back door.

Dawn reached into a pocket, pulled out the four-inch wad of thousand and hundred dollar bills she had taken from the drug dealer's pocket, and handed a third of the bills to Abe. "I'm sorry to bring this down on you," Dawn said. "You'd better get outta here and start again in another space. I know you've done it before."

"I'll survive," Abe said, weeping at the sight of the dead woman by the door. "How could they kill like this?"

Dawn had no answer. "Take care of yourself, Dawn," Abe said, putting a hand on her shoulder. "I'll be praying for you."

Within seconds, Dawn was inching up behind Winston on the rope. With both of their backpacks, it was more strenuous for him than the climbing workouts he and Dawn had practiced together in the Resistance camp. At the time he had thought they were just staying in shape. He now realized that she had been preparing for their escape all along.

"Follow me and stay low," she warned, as she arrived behind him on the rooftop. The huge duffel bag on her back had barely slowed her down. She untied the rope from the ventilation fan and coiled it back up in her hands. Winston noticed her face was drenched with sweat.

Hunched over, Dawn led him back over a half-dozen rooftops. They jumped down to a roof one storey below. "Hit the ground here and cover your head till I give the signal," Dawn ordered.

Winston watched her move to the fortified roof door. She pulled a small square of plastic explosive from a pouch on her belt, turned a timer, and stuck it against the wall perpendicular to the doorway. She rushed back to the ground next to Winston, cupping her head in her arms just as a dull thud blew a two-foot hole in the wall.

Dawn shimmied through the hole before the dust had settled. Once inside, she unlocked the door and swung it open. "Down here," she whispered urgently, grabbing the duffel bag and carrying it down to the hall landing one flight below.

Dawn unlatched the duffel and carefully laid its contents on the floor. Winston was amazed at how much gear she had squeezed into one bag. "Take off your jacket and clothes, leave your underwear," she instructed, as she tore hers off and threw them in a pile nearby. "This is a commercial building, a store below and offices up here. No one should be here on a Sunday. Still, the troopers will be searching the buildings around the soup kitchen, so we have to hurry. Put on the larger wetsuit, it'll keep you warm later. I'll dress you from there."

"Wetsuit?" Winston looked at the stuff Dawn had laid all over the floor. She grabbed the smaller of two wetsuits on the ground and started dressing. He did the same. "Are we heading into the sewers next?"

"I'm sorry there's been so little time to talk. I wish I had laid out the escape plans with you sooner, but I thought we'd have more time."

"No time like the present," Winston smiled, thinking how sexy she looked in the form-fitting wetsuit.

"Stand still, right here. Quinn and his crew worked with me on this outfit for months. Hold your arms out."

Dawn tightened a titanium hoop that had fallen around Winston's waist, then adjusted the arms that extended out from it to form a four-foot wide frame that started below his waist.

"Quinn called this his indestructible body tube," Dawn explained. "Said he'd been scheming to build one since he was twelve. I'm putting an oxygen tank, water pouch, and tubes into the back frame now. All Quinn's design. But it was my idea to have it double as a fatso disguise."

"A what?"

"We'll be disguised as fat Samoans, and I picked up just the sort of clothes that big people wear to give their bodies room. I was working on this the whole time you were revising the script. Put your arms in this, then step into these pants."

The enormous bright cotton outfit felt like a tent hanging from the titanium frame that rested on Winston's shoulders. He stepped awkwardly into the huge-waisted pants. Dawn tied the drawstring closed.

"The tubes for the air and water will be right beneath your neck. We won't need them until we get put into the garbage bags."

"The garbage bags?"

"I know this is going to sound freaky, but you've got to trust me on this. I've gotten you this far."

"You're right," Winston said. "I'd be dead meat without you."

"Funny you should bring up dead meat," Dawn said, laying the other titanium suit around herself. "That's what we're going to be smuggled out of this country as. I've got a good friend who owns a meat wholesaler in the ghetto. They get deliveries early morning, carve up the carcasses, then load the waste product into a collection truck around nine or ten, even on Sundays. The truck picks up from the other Bed-Stuy meat wholesalers, then hauls it to a pier outside the ghetto. It gets dumped onto a barge, along with truckloads of waste from all the other meat wholesalers in the city."

"So we get put in a garbage bag with meat carcasses and dumped on a barge?"

"Right. Then the barge heads up to a fertilizer mill up in Plattsburgh, and left for a few hours. That's when we jump ship and swim twenty miles to Canada. That's what the wetsuits are for."

"You've got this figured out?"

"Every step of it."

"That's all I need to know. Just don't leave me behind."

"There are a half dozen nutrition bars in the pouch around your side. Some other stuff, too, that we'll need later. Now I'm gonna pull over the mask, and it'll be goodbye, handsome. But first . . ."

She placed her hands on his cheeks and kissed him passionately. He wanted her right there. "Mmmm," she said, pulling away and staring into his eyes. "I'd never leave you behind, you sexy thing."

She carefully pulled a form-fitting mask over his face. He remembered being fit for the masks in October, thinking it was for Halloween. He had no idea what he looked like, but guessed he didn't appear very different from Dawn. Long black hair, dark skin, heavy double chin, wide shoulders, heavy chest and an enormous belly and butt. A long flowing yellow and orange native shirt, and drawstring pants to match.

Dawn handed him his small backpack and a cane. "We each take our small packs and canes into the garbage bags with us. We'll need them later."

Dawn started down the stairs. Winston tried to follow. He stumbled and caught himself on the handrail.

"Lean on the handrail," Dawn advised. "This'll take some getting used to. Use the cane when we get outside. Go slow, it'll be more of a waddle than a walk. It's nearly a mile away, so it'll take us almost an hour."

They got downstairs and exited onto the sidewalk. Daylight had just arrived. Shops were rolling up their heavy steel grates and people were heading to work at their Bed-Stuy jobs. Many of the ghetto residents were recently-arrived immigrants. Enough of them wore their native costumes that the two Samoan men who waddled steadily forward on their canes did not seem out of place.

Winston looked around through the slits in his snug-fitting mask. Homeland Security urban riot vehicles were on every other street, camera towers in the air recording and viewing the faces of hundreds of people all around them. Undercover marshals and bounty hunters in flak jackets stood on many street corners looking people over and aggressively stopping pedestrians to show them "Wanted" posters.

Winston noticed a de-commissioned Predator drone plummeting toward the ground a few blocks away. It landed with a sharp whack as it smashed harmlessly through the roof of a parked car. This meant, he realized, that the ghetto's widely deployed anti-drone defenses had survived the destruction of their Resistance camp. It also meant that Homeland Security was trying everything to kill him.

They had been walking slowly for just ten minutes when a

pair of goonish bounty hunters accosted them on a street corner. One waved an automatic pistol while showing them the poster offering the five million dollar reward for Winston Smith.

"You seen him—we split reward for info?" the goon demanded menacingly, while his partner held up another poster. Winston was nervous that they would notice his mask, but shook his head convincingly, and kept moving. The bounty hunters immediately shifted their focus to a few pedestrians walking behind them. "You seen him—we split reward for info?" he repeated.

Uniformed Homeland Security troopers were out, as well, walking in six-man squads through the streets, stopping vehicles at gunpoint for spot checks.

"That's an unusual sight," Dawn remarked, as they walked. "Usually they're afraid of snipers taking potshots at them. Good thing they're not checking people for IDs. Quarter of the people in Bed-Stuy don't have them, another quarter are wanted for something on the outside. They'd have an armed uprising for sure if they tried that one. Still, I wouldn't want to be this guy Smith."

Winston was reminded that Dawn believed that any conversation or appearance anywhere outside of the Resistance camp might be monitored at any time. "Don't you know," she had told him just a few days earlier, "the killers are in control."

After more than an hour of slow, laborious plodding, they arrived at a block crammed with large refrigerated trucks. Workers unloaded huge red carcasses of cows and pigs onto carts and outdoor meat hooks.

Dawn led Winston into one of the busy loading areas of the meat wholesalers. "Carmen around?" she asked a workman, doing her best to sound like a Samoan man. The man pointed to a doorway curtained with thick plastic ribbons.

They entered the refrigerated cutting room. Inside, a squat, sturdy young man in a long apron leaned over a long table cutting a cow carcass with a table saw. He set usable pieces on a rolling tray, and tossed the excess fat and bones into a large bag-lined garbage bin on wheels.

"Hey, Carmen," Dawn called out, over the din of the saw.

Carmen noticed them and turned off the saw. "Who the fuck are you?" he asked, quickly grabbing a long knife in each hand. "Keep your arms where I can see them and don't make any fast moves, or I'll—"

"Chill out, Carmen. It's me, Dawn."

Carmen recognized the voice and squinted, then broke into a wide smile. "Man, that's a great disguise. You really know how to carry it off. Good thing, too, with troopers thick as flies out there. They're looking for the guy who was interviewed during that simulcast—"

"I know," said Dawn, scanning the large room to make sure they were alone. "Listen, time is short. Remember that big favor I talked to you about last month?"

Carmen nodded and looked at the masked person standing next to her. "Right. You said there'd be two of you, in disguise."

"Can we do it now?"

"Now?"

"Right now."

Carmen walked to the entrance and watched the loading bay through the hanging plastic strips. "The waste truck picks up around nine o'clock, barge takes off at noon."

"You still the top load?" Dawn asked.

"I hear we are. I haven't been to the barge for years. But Bed-Stuy generally goes last for everything, so I imagine nothing's changed."

Carmen made another nervous glance out onto the loading dock, then grabbed a rolling bin and brought it near Dawn. "Make it fast," he urged, laying a thick black plastic bag into the bin. "Climb in, yell all clear when you close up the protective suit I'm assuming is under that crazy outfit. I'll hit the bagging button and you'll be on your way outta here with the rest of our garbage."

"My friend first," Dawn insisted, helping Winston climb onto the cutting table and lowering him into a bin. She pulled the long shirt off him, and stretched a head extension from his shoulder frame. Carmen resumed his lookout in the doorway.

"You'll be able to take the mask off and move your hands within the titanium skeleton," Dawn explained as she adjusted Winston's suit within the bin. "I've put your cane in the frame around your back. You'll know we've arrived when we've stopped for more than a half hour. Feel this control in the suit here . . . switch it here, and a mini-drill will bore through and eject a thin steel cable with an air hose in it to the top of the bag pile. A built-in compressor will bring air into your bag. When we arrive, switch it like this, and the 'spider claw' will spread out and pull your bag to the top of the heap. A small knife in the suit's belt will allow you to cut open the bag when it's time to get out."

"A 'spider claw?'" Winston tried to picture it all in his mind. "Where will you be?"

"Doing the same thing and meeting you on top, I hope, for a long swim. There'll be some air in the bag to start, use it till it runs thin. You can peel off the mask once the barge gets moving, then take air from the tube near your neck, and water from the other tube. The food bars are in your waist pouch. Ready?"

"As ready as I'll ever be," Winston said. "But that's not saying much."

"Hit it, Carmen," Dawn said.

Carmen wheeled the bin to a bagging machine that sealed the bag shut, lifted it out, and dumped it on a conveyor belt to the loading dock.

"My turn," Dawn said. Carmen put another bag in the empty bin and returned it to the cutting table. Dawn fixed her head extension.

"You sure that thing's gonna work?" Carmen asked, wheeling her to the bag-loading machine. "The bags landing on top of you in the truck and on the barge could weigh half a ton."

"Shouldn't be a problem," Dawn yelled, from inside the bin. "Thanks, Carmen."

"I owed you one," Carmen said, hitting the bagging button.

Despite his fatigue, Winston was restless inside the thick black plastic bag. He heard Dawn's bag land on top of his with a thud, and was relieved that his frame didn't budge. A short while later, he heard another bag land in the bin, then another. He peeled off his mask, took a sip of water, and waited.

The garbage truck arrived. Its hydraulic arm roughly lifted Winston's container and dumped its contents into its hold. The truck pulled out, drove to a loading dock nearby, and picked up another load.

The garbage truck made two more pickups, then headed steadily through the ghetto streets. It was loud and dark in the bag, and the starting and stopping were constant. Winston pictured the truck driving along the Brooklyn waterfront. Only nine months ago, he thought, he had left the city on a first-class plane ticket to London. Now he was in the belly of a garbage truck loaded with cow and pig bones, heading to Plattsburgh. Where the fuck is Plattsburgh, anyway, he asked himself.

A half hour later, the truck stopped. A deafening engine started below him, and he felt the truck body being lifted high into the air. One end of the truck dropped to a forty-five-degree angle, sending the sealed bags of meat waste tumbling into the open barge.

The rolling of his bag left Winston dizzy, but grateful that his frame held. He pictured dozens of bags falling around his. One of them held Dawn.

The barge started up. Well, Winston thought, we'll either be shipped off to freedom or buried alive. The odds of survival seemed better on the barge than in the ghetto, with a five million dollar price on his head.

Twenty-Seven

The small engine in Winston's escape suit purred to a stop. He had grabbed hold of the knife in his waist pouch a while earlier, not realizing how painfully slowly the small motor that pulled his bag to the top of the heap would work. When he flicked the switch, he had pictured expanding spider-leg-like talons opening up to grip the bags around it on the top of the open barge, and had assumed that it would use its steel cable to pull his bag to the top of the heap in just a few minutes.

Winston sliced the thick black plastic bag open, crawled out of his escape suit, and emerged cautiously into the dark, cool early morning. Resting on his knees, he looked around to make sure nobody had spotted him. The barge's engine room was still, and there were no lights anywhere. He stood slowly, stretching his cramped body, noticing the stars as they glittered brilliantly over Lake Champlain.

He heard a rumbling under the mountain of bags twenty feet away. Crouching low, he walked over and watched Dawn's bag emerge, displacing the piles around it. He told her the deck was clear, and before he knew it, she was stretching out right nearby.

"I hope you got some sleep?" Dawn asked, pleased that the escape suit had worked so well. "Because we've got a looooooong swim ahead, and need to disappear from here real quickly."

Winston nodded, eager to escape the stench. He helped her fold and strap their titanium suits and disguise clothes with the steel cable. She laid their other gear in two waterproof bags, and put their scuba equipment and oxygen tanks into a net bag. She had rigged a water-ski bar to a small battery-powered aqua motor, and showed him where they would both hold the bar.

"We'll be going more than twenty miles, all of it underwater," she explained. "We'll need to supplement the motor with our leg power. Our mini-flippers will help some. I've got the light and map, so I'll navigate. Meet you in the water."

Dawn tossed the bags and excess gear over the side of the barge, and jumped in. Winston hit the water a few seconds later. They swam to the deserted shore nearby, and helped one another adjust their small tanks, fins, and bags. Dawn found a large rock, which she strapped to the excess gear. They swam with it to deeper water, dropped it to the bottom, and started the small aqua motor.

The powerful lithium battery lasted for the three-hour underwater journey as they traveled along Lake Champlain, finally crossing to Canada through the Richelieu River.

Dawn used a small periscope to check out the area before they surfaced on the muddy banks of the river in southern Quebec, five miles north of the New York border. They found a spot in a thicket of trees to peel off their wetsuits. Before Dawn changed into the warm travel clothes from her bag, she carefully strapped their scuba equipment, wetsuits and waterproof bags to a rock, swam the bundle back into the frigid water, and let it sink to the bottom.

Winston helped pat her dry with a bandana and rubbed her body to help warm it. They finished dressing while snacking on nutrition bars and what little drinking water they had left. Dawn applied a fake beard to Winston's face with spirit gum. While they packed their remaining gear they had kept into small daypacks, she smiled at him confidently. "Welcome to Canada, Mr. Smith."

They embraced, and Winston didn't want to let her go. In just six months, Dawn had gone from an unwashed warrior to his most trusted friend, lover and protector. "Let's make love right here to commemorate our escape," he urged.

"We're not there yet, gorgeous," she said. "We need to get to a safer place."

"We are in a safer place," Winston protested. "We're in Canada. It's a free country. We can apply for asylum and do and say whatever we want."

"Just because we're in Canada doesn't mean we're safe. We're still just five miles from the border. There are regiments of marshals and bounty hunters posing as tourists, besides hundreds of locals who make their living hunting down American escapees with prices on their heads. You're the biggest prize that ever made it through the border."

"I thought Canada was refusing to extradite Americans who weren't violent felons."

"Who said anything about the Canadian government? Flouting international law in pursuit of anyone General Bashcrost can construe as part of the War on Terror—and that covers absolutely anyone—has been one of the proud tenets of this Administration. You must have heard of their 'Hot Pursuit' doctrine?"

Dawn started walking toward a small road that ran alongside the river bank near the town of Lacolle. Winston followed, frustrated. "I thought that just applied in countries we're at war with."

"Remember what you told me that you and Paul witnessed in London? That goes on all the time in Canada. Only here, they've got Harrier jets and Apache helicopters to pop over and transport the Homeland Security marshals or bounty hunters or prisoners or dead bodies that they don't feel like burying locally."

"Why would Canada stand for it?"

"What choice do they have? They try to beef up their border patrols, stop marshals from carrying guns across the borders, even challenge the occasional American air raid with their own planes. When the raids get through or Canadians become 'collateral damage,' the Canadian government complains to the United Nations, where it's like, 'Take a number.' Blush pulled America out of the U.N. eight years ago. They pay off anyone they need locally, drug or shoot whoever gets in their way, all part of their 'doctrine' of going after the 'bad guys.'"

"So now anything goes, whatever country I escape to, because I'm one of the bad guys?"

"Welcome to the club," Dawn said.

They walked for half an hour along the shoulder of the sleepy road, turning their heads and shielding their faces from the few cars that passed, ostensibly blocking dust and pebbles from their eyes. Dawn kept glancing along the waterfront area until she saw what she was looking for.

"Walk with me," she said, leading him on a tree-lined trail to the riverbank. "Wait here and don't let them see your face," she instructed as they got near an area where a few small docks reached into the river. Two teenaged boys were sitting on the end of the dock, fishing and smoking pot. Their bicycles lay on the nearby shore.

Dawn walked out on the pier and playfully pointed in Winston's direction. "My Canadian boyfriend over there made a bet with me that you money-hating Canadian guys wouldn't sell us your two bicycles, no matter how many of my filthy American dollars I offered." Dawn pulled a bunch of bills from a pocket where she had put the money she took from the drug dealer. "I'd like to prove him wrong with, say, two thousand American dollars."

"Maybe he's right about us Canadian guys," the bolder of the teens said, looking her and the money over carefully. "Maybe it'd cost you three thousand of your American dollars to win that bet."

"Done," Dawn smiled. She gave them the cash, wheeled the bikes to Winston, and minutes later, they were pedaling along the road.

"Neat trick," Winston said.

"You ain't seen nothing yet," Dawn said, over her shoulder.

They cycled along the quiet road. Dawn stopped to look at a flyer taped to a telephone pole. It was a Wanted poster for Winston, with a local number to call, and a promise to share a five million dollar reward.

"This isn't a good sign," she said, as they started riding. "Good thing the turkey in that picture doesn't exactly look like you."

Winston found nothing to laugh at. The chase and swim and constant movement were wearing him out. "So we going to pedal all the way to Montreal?"

"Montreal is too risky. So is trying to contact the Montreal Resistance to get a ride, or shelter. Homeland Security uses the National Security Agency to monitor any calls they want, wherever they happen in the world. So the Resistance lines will all be bugged. Worse, the reward on you is high, and well publicized. It could tempt someone, even someone who didn't like our government. We can't take chances with strangers."

"So we're going to camp in the forests and eat nuts and berries?"

"We're going to Vancouver."

"We're cycling to Vancouver? It's thousands of miles!"

"Relax," Dawn advised. "Enjoy the ride. I'll get you there."

They biked for a few more hours, through increasingly larger towns, until Dawn pulled over in back of a large gas station.

"Okay, we're far enough from the border towns now," she said. "Watch the bikes and bags and wait here."

Twenty-five minutes later, a dusty Subaru pulled up next to Winston. "Get in," Dawn called through her open window. "Leave the bikes."

Winston threw their bags into the back seat and climbed in.

"Nice car," he said. "Did you steal it?"

"All we need is to get arrested and deported. I used my legal tender to get this legal tender." Driving on, she tossed a signed car title onto Winston's lap, along with a hand-written authorization to drive the car using the seller's insurance for one week. "It took me so long because I had to find someone who carried their title with them."

"Why would someone sell you their car at a gas station?"

"I gave him eighty thousand good reasons to sell me his car," Dawn smiled. "These Canadians might not have any respect left for the American government, but they still respect our green-backs."

The drive across Canada, along side roads, took eight days. Within hours of setting out, Dawn arranged for a body shop to paint the car a different color, paying double for a rush job and leaving Winston in a nearby park. They later stopped to buy camping gear, food, and a few good maps. They slept and made love in campgrounds along the way. Taking no chances, Winston wore sunglasses everywhere they went, and buried his face in a map whenever they stopped for gas.

They arrived in Vancouver, ditched the car, and caught a bus to the apartment of an old friend of Dawn's who was part of the city's large expatriate Resistance community. That evening at a huge outdoor party they celebrated the New Year and their new life together in a free country.

TWENTY-EIGHT

As God's United States entered 2015, the government attempted to crush any response to the Resistance's simulcast. Under the ruthless command of General John Bashcrost, every federal law enforcement and intelligence agency worked overtime to raid one urban ghetto after another, arresting and killing thousands. The Ministry of Truth doubled the rotation of its public service ads, reminding citizens that the Constitution forbade treasonous speech in the home, workplace, schools, or public places, and that Homeland Security was watching and listening at all times.

Rewards for Patriotic Citizens who reported suspected "Hate America" speech were tripled, with special bonuses offered for turning in family members. The Homeland Security Tip lines were busy day and night. Channel Always-On carried mandatory simulcasts each evening, and stayed in "monitor" mode twenty-four hours a day, to "ensure that subversive activity would be detected early and effectively."

New arrests of citizens once considered patriotic reached

heights not seen since the waves of mass arrests in 2006 and 2010. Tents sprung up like mushrooms in thousands of prison labor camps across the country to accommodate more than two million new convicts during the first three months of the year.

The Resistance burrowed further underground, while its expatriate membership swelled. Emigration to Canada, Europe, and Latin America increased as citizens heeded the Resistance call to leave the country and change their government from the outside. Newspapers in Canada and Europe began reporting increases in American amnesty applications of six to nine hundred percent.

During the first two months of the New Year, the Vancouver Resistance community that Dawn and Winston had joined doubled in size, to more than ten thousand members. With its progressive local government and proximity to America's northwest, Vancouver had already been a hub of the International Resistance media effort. With Dawn and Winston joining the effort, its role grew even larger.

Canadian techies worked with expatriates and young hackers around the world to expand their knowledge base far beyond an untraceable communication network. Teen renegades led by Quinn's group had orchestrated the satellite hijacking, and hackers everywhere were emboldened by their success. By March, they presented their Direct Action counterparts with a means of continuing the media war launched by the successful simulcast.

They called it their "spawn of spam" technology. Using hijacked servers, they were able to send an untraceable daily video e-mail to every computer in God's United States. The v-mail packet would open every time any new e-mail was checked, and it could not be shut down.

Once Winston had recovered from two successful plastic surgery procedures, he began collaborating with Dawn to provide direction to the Resistance media group. They helped create a series of commercials for delivery through the v-mail spam system. On the first day of spring, the new campaign began.

Across God's United States, people logged into their computers and found themselves forced to watch a sixty-second ad showing public demonstrations and open elections in countries around the world, with the question, "What Happened to Democracy At Home?" The next day they were greeted with images of happy Americans living in Mexico and Costa Rica with the slogan, "Had Enough Yet? We're Waiting for You." The next few weeks carried updates of the "Top Ten Tips for Everyday Resistance," including one that encouraged Americans to open offshore bank accounts to make it easier when they emigrated. "It's Your Right!" the ad noted, "Two million Nationalist Party members with secret foreign bank accounts can't be wrong."

The growth of the International Resistance movement picked up speed. Famous American performers and athletes applied for amnesty while on foreign tours, and then spoke out at concerts to criticize the Blush government and its endless wars. News footage of their appearances made its way into the v-mail spam. Every time Homeland Security's technology experts created a patch to stop the "treasonous virus," it evolved into a new form, and was back delivering dissident propaganda to America's computer screens the next day.

Winston started by working behind the scenes, but his experience propelled him to the forefront of the media campaigns. He and Dawn developed the idea for two dozen simultaneous benefit concerts in major cities worldwide on behalf of the victims of the Blush Administration's wars. They called it the "Another World is Possible" benefit. News coverage of the concerts attracted millions of students around the globe to the cause. It was followed by an international boycott of American products produced in prison labor camps, a call for international sanctions against God's United States for war crimes, and the introduction of spontaneous mass "peace waves" at sporting events around the world.

Winston and Dawn assumed new identities and settled into a small, non-descript apartment in a building managed by a member of the Resistance. They never ventured out of the city. Making sure they handled all communication from the safe computers at the secret

Resistance offices, they shunned private telephones for security.

One evening as summer approached, Winston returned home with Dawn from the office and confessed that he had used the Resistance's anonymous web servers to make a personal voice call for the first time.

"I haven't spoken with my mother in years," he said, as they prepared dinner together. "I wanted her to know that I'm still alive. Don't worry—I.T. assured me it was untraceable."

"I guess Homeland Security knows you're alive somewhere anyway. All they'd get is a recording of your voice from the N.S.A. intercept. What'd you say to her?"

"That I was in Denmark," Winston grinned.

"Good lie. Keep old man Bashcrost guessing."

"That I was sorry for blocking her calls all these years. And that I've never been happier in my life." Winston grabbed Dawn from behind and bit the back of her neck.

"Sounds like a good first conversation. How's she doing?"

"She says she loved the *1984* movie, as well my interview and ads. Said the expat community in Costa Rica is growing like crazy and has never been so stirred up. Said she's proud of her only son."

"I'm glad you're back in touch with her."

"While we're on the subject of being back in touch . . . I also made a voice call to Lilly."

"You what?"

"Hey, you just agreed voice calls were safe."

"And what did *she* say, your dancing princess?" Dawn edged away from him, trying to hide her concern.

"Don't tell me you're jealous about a woman I haven't even seen or spoken with for more than a year!"

"Why did you call her?"

"Does being in the Resistance movement mean we can't care about other people anymore?"

"I'm sure she's doing fine, living it up in your fancy Fifth Avenue penthouse."

"You've got no idea how she's doing. Neither did I, which is why I called."

Dawn saw he was upset. "I see what you mean," she said, restraining herself. "So how is she doing?"

"Badly. She couldn't say much over the web phone, but she sounded terrible, and said she wants to see me one last time."

"She what? You told her about us, didn't you?"

"Of course I did. I said she should forget about me, that I've found someone, someone . . . someone I want to be with forever."

Dawn's face softened. "You told her that, huh? Might help if you told *me* that every now and then."

He drew her close to him. "This isn't about me wanting to be with another woman. It's about worrying over the mess I've left behind."

"I understand," Dawn said. "I hope you explained how impossible it would be to meet, with the bounty hunters and all."

"Uhhhm . . . actually, I started with that. But she's desperate for closure. Her first and greatest love dumped her with a phone call. The first day she moved in, she made me swear to her that I'd never break up over the phone."

"Things have changed. Both your lives would be in danger if she came to Canada to see you. She's got to understand that."

"She doesn't."

"Don't even think of it," Dawn fumed. She backed away, so angry she couldn't even look at him. "I rescued you so you could live, not throw your life away because you don't want to hurt some bimbo's feelings!"

Winston tried a quick exit. "I'm either going to do the right thing here or not. Sometimes moral action is about trust."

"Sometimes it's about stupidity."

"What is this really about?" Winston asked accusingly. "Is this about jealousy?"

"Fuck that," Dawn cursed. "It's about survival, you idiot, it's about a million fucken killers out there looking to win the lottery by whacking your dissident ass. Call her back. We can go to an Internet café right now and rig a voice-only call."

Winston shook his head. "She'll be across the border in four days. We can wait at least that long to arrange a meeting. That'll give us plenty of time for a security plan."

"Please, Winston. I have . . . I have a bad feeling about this."

"What are you really worried about? That she'll ask for asylum and stay with me and you and I will be over?"

"Not at all. I worry that it's a trap and they'll take you from me like they took . . ." she broke down sobbing.

"I'm not your father being drafted and sent to Pakistan, and I'm not your mother being arrested by Homeland Security at a demonstration. We're in Canada, you've got us here safely. I told her she should fly to Toronto, go to a library, open an offshore e-mail account, and be prepared to travel. I gave her an offshore sleeper e-mail address that I can check without a trace. She won't even know I'm in Vancouver until she gets to Canada."

"I . . . I don't want to lose you," Dawn said, moving close to him again.

"I'm not going anywhere."

For a few moments, Dawn considered knocking him out and tying him up for a week, until Lilly's visit was over. It would be for his own good, she thought. But she would have to deal with him when he came to. He could always contact Lilly again, and next time, he might even want her to stay.

Dawn realized she had no choice but to arrange for the most secure rendezvous possible. She consulted with Winston and their new friends in the Vancouver Resistance community. They chose a large, popular restaurant downtown, and organized a plan that would allow as many safeguards as possible.

A week later, with all the pieces in place, a few volunteers from their Resistance cell met Lilly at Vancouver's main post office. They brought her to their car, removed her phone and dropped it into a lead box, and carefully checked her for electronic bugs or tracking devices. Then they drove her to a restaurant at the far end of the city. They told her she would be meeting Winston soon, but that he wanted her to order lunch and start without him.

Lilly waited for more than an hour, poking at her food, perplexed, while her escorts monitored her and the approaching roads. When they were satisfied the area was clear, they returned to Lilly's table, and told her that Winston would be meeting her at an entirely different place. Making sure they weren't being followed, they circled the city again and ended up in a different neighborhood. They escorted Lilly into a bustling restaurant called "Organic Delight," apologized for the security protocol, and told her that Winston would be arriving soon. They sat her at a window table and watched her from their surveillance car double-parked across the street.

Twenty minutes later, Winston's driver dropped him off at Organic Delight and parked nearby.

A hostess brought Winston through the crowded restaurant to Lilly's table. She stood to greet him, looking flustered and a bit confused. His plastic surgery-altered face was unfamiliar, but his voice was reassuring.

In the year since Winston had last seen her, Lilly had grown thinner. He could see the stress in her face, and felt guilty thinking that he was responsible for it. He kissed her cheek and hugged her tightly.

"Thank you for doing this," she smiled gratefully, as they both sat down. "I'm just . . . I'm just so sorry."

"I'm the one who should be sorry," Winston said. "You never signed on for this. Homeland Security must be making your life miserable."

Lilly broke down and started crying uncontrollably. She dabbed her face with her napkin, trying to calm down. "I can't help crying, I must look awful," she said. "This isn't the way I want it to end, me looking like this. I—I have to go to the bathroom and wash up, I feel like a disaster."

"You look great," Winston lied. "But go ahead, you've been traveling. I'll order you a surprise."

"Thanks," Lilly said, pressing his hand. "You're so sweet. I'm really sorry."

She walked to the bathroom in the back of the restaurant. Winston looked over the menu for the first time and tried to attract the waiter's attention.

He appreciated the moments alone. He wished she wasn't so broken up.

Winston suddenly felt nervous and looked at his phone. It had somehow shut itself off. He tried to turn it on as the lights in the restaurant dimmed, then blacked out. He jumped out of his seat, but it was too late.

Four Homeland Security S.W.A.T. teams arrived simultaneously from four directions, leading with their assault rifles. One six-man team came through the front door, another through the back, and two teams smashed through the restaurant's quaint, wood-framed windows, sending shattered glass and fragments of wood everywhere.

"Everyone, hands in front of you and down to the floor, now!" the troopers shouted, "Everyone down, this is your last warning!"

Winston's body was covered by a dozen strategically aimed red laser sights. He stretched his hands in front of him and laid himself face down on the floor.

One diner hesitated, a fashionably dressed, athletic man in his fifties who was sitting with his wife and two daughters. "Now wait one minute," the man said, holding up a scolding finger and standing his ground. "This is Canada, you can't just—"

The man's body was cut in half by a barrage of large caliber bullets, splashing blood all over the table.

"Stop! Stop! Stop!" Winston yelled from the floor, his voice drowned out by the sound of screams and gunfire as three powerful tranquilizer darts were shot into his body.

Twenty-nine

our months later, Winston sat on a stool in a large television studio and stared blankly out the window. His thoughts had become a kaleidoscope of emotions, mixed together to form colors. They were different than the colors he could see out the window, the soft color of the sky, the tree dancing in the breeze. He liked the colors there, not the ones he saw when he closed his eyes, not the ones in his kaleidoscope.

Winston wanted to remember the names of the colors, but they would not come to him. He had once known them, he realized. He tried to access the memory. This made his head ache terribly. The question disappeared, leaving him with a feeling of relief. A bird flew past and he smiled.

"Can you read what you see in the teleprompter for us, Winston?" a loud, authoritative voice asked.

That must be my name, Winston realized. The helpful person had told him his name and asked whether he could read.

Text appeared on a teleprompter screen in front of him. "My

fellow Americans," Winston read carefully, proud of his ability to say the words on the screen. "I am here tonight to ask forgiveness. First the forgiveness of our God, and of our Lord Jesus—"

"Very good, Winston," the voice, from a nearby amplifier, interrupted. "Read it again, from the beginning, but this time, please try to speak a lot louder."

Whose voice was that, Winston asked himself, sensing something familiar. An intense pain swept through his head for a few seconds, then disappeared. What had he just been told to do, he wondered.

"A lot louder, this time," the voice reminded him.

"Right," Winston said. "I can do that." The words on the screen appeared again. He read them loudly. It was easy.

Neil Swan switched off the microphone in the White House meeting room. He nodded as Winston read the speech he had written from a gigantic video monitor. It was not his first closed-door meeting with the President, Vice President, and Homeland Security General, but it was easily the most nerve-wracking.

"So that's the great and powerful Oz," President George Blush observed, pacing the room while watching the screen. "Looks like a dim-witted little prick to me."

"He's certainly been taken down a peg, Mr. President," Vice President Dick Croney assured him. "Good thing that we have a Homeland Security General who's willing to apply the pharmaco-logical anti-terrorist tools that our new constitution gives us."

"This battle will be over soon," Homeland Security General John Bashcrost said assuredly. "We've terminated Resistance cells in eight ghettos and arrested more than fifty thousand Resistance aiders and abettors in the last nine months alone. They won't be coming back." His eyes darted to President Blush, who nodded his approval. "This thing will fall apart soon as we round up the last of these isolated terrorist-financed trouble-makers. Everyone else will calm down, especially after we have our little fairy sing a new tune."

The President laughed. "Imagine this retarded scumbag hijacking our emergency Always-On channel for more than three hours. How the hell did he do it?"

"I'm sure he had helpers," Minister of Truth Russ Limetoff chimed in. "We've got to continue to grow our domestic surveillance efforts."

"We've got to stay the course," Croney urged. "That's why we can't let the Party-sponsored bill to increase funding for Hullibarton's privatization of our immigration agency languish any longer."

"One day at a time," President Blush counseled. "Budget talks every other Monday only—you guys promised."

"Yes sir, Mr. President," Croney replied.

President Blush watched as Winston got off the stool and started to wander away. A team of government handlers quickly pulled him back to his stool. "Look at this guy—what a pathetic loser. You should have brought him down long ago, Swan."

Neil Swan stepped forward, his round face reddened. "I'm sorry, Mr. President. Sir, you are absolutely right. Although as his record reflects, his work had always been patriotic before this. Perhaps it's the price we pay for allowing freedom to travel to treasonous countries like England. The BBC probably got to him with drugs."

"But we're getting him back, aren't we, Neil?" Russ Limetoff tried to smirk, but his face twitched uncontrollably instead. Embarrassed, he bent down and pretended to tie a shoelace. The satellite hijacking and the subsequent mushrooming of dissent and emigration had created the first crisis in his career with the Blush Administration. The pressure had forced him to triple his daily dosage of OxyContin, and the side effects of the narcotic had unleashed their own set of problems. He wished that it was as simple as putting a bullet in Winston's head and moving on. But that would not counter the damage that had already been done.

"We sure are, Russ," Swan replied, trying to sound confident.

"We've got the right drugs, the right people, and the right script for tomorrow's simulcast. This terrorist will be setting the record straight, I can assure you of that."

"It looks like he's having trouble just reading the damned teleprompter," President Blush complained. "How do we know he won't fuck it all up tomorrow?"

Russ Limetoff looked to his subordinate, Neil Swan, for an answer. "We've already got two successful run-throughs in eight tries," Swan explained. "Our people will stay at it, through the night if need be, until they get three good ones in a row. Then we'll just add make-up, and march him out for the cameras. Of course we'll pre-record the simulcast, which means if he stumbles a bit in the first taping, we can do it over."

"Why can't you just get it right the first time?" the President demanded.

"Of course, sir. That's what we plan. But . . . well . . . you know me, gentlemen, and you know that I've never been a hymie whiner. Still, I need to remind you that the Ministry of Truth only administers the drugs that Homeland Security's R&D department creates. We were told that this new pharmaceutical would simply make wrong-thinkers impressionable. But it seems to have completely removed Smith's ability to reason."

"Is that why you couldn't get any useful information out of him about that Vancouver Resistance?" Vice President Croney asked, looking accusingly at the Homeland Security General.

"The drug cocktail we created for this terrorist was more . . . potent than anticipated, I acknowledge that," Bashcrost replied defensively. "But that sword will cut both ways. We've got him scheduled as a monthly guest on O'Manley's show. We'll be trotting him out to renounce and denounce and accuse for as long as we want. His 'fellow travelers' will know he's the real deal because his voice prints will match his BBC interview, and his present condition will be a visceral deterrent to those thinking of crossing us in the future."

"Well, as long as he can read the teleprompter tomorrow, and whenever else we want him to, his mental happiness sure ain't our problem," Russ Limetoff said. "He may be a vegetable, but at least he's our vegetable."

General Bashcrost joined his colleagues in a round of laughter. "Russ, you are one funny rascal."

"That's our Russ," Vice President Croney agreed. "The sickest puppy in the litter—and the most effective."

Early the next morning, three men in neat uniforms arrived in Winston's room with a beautiful suit of new clothes for him to wear. One of them patiently managed his necktie, and even applied shiny gel to his messy hair.

"You'll come with us," the uniformed man said. "There will be lots of people where we're going. Important people. There will be a teleprompter. Like yesterday. We'll practice first. Then you'll read in your loudest and proudest voice."

Winston did not understand what he meant by important people, or what happened yesterday. But he wanted to follow the man and do what he said. The man was strong, handsome, and very helpful. Whatever he would be told to do, he would get to practice first. That felt like a good thing.

Winston followed the uniformed men into the back of a long black car, where more men, even bigger men, waited for him. They wore shiny boots and crisply pressed uniforms. Nobody said anything. He enjoyed watching the flashing lights and listening to the sirens. The long car went very fast. There were more cars in front of them, also with flashing lights and sirens. Winston smiled and looked out the window.

The caravan drove through a high black gate that swung inward as they arrived. Someone opened the car door and he followed the helpful man into a very big white house.

The helpers led Winston into a room. It was a big room, with lots of empty chairs, and a stage. A woman put makeup on his face. Then he was brought to the stage, and asked to read the words in front of him. He started to read. It made him proud that he could read like that. One of the uniformed men interrupted him, and asked him to read louder. The words appeared again. It was easy to read louder.

Soon more people entered the room, many of them with cameras and other equipment that they busily set up. He wondered what they were all doing there, so busy. A helpful man in a uniform offered him a seat while he waited. He did not know what he was waiting for, but it felt good to sit down.

Although she was still in Canada, Dawn was able to watch the special American Homeland Security simulcast in her living room on the international Foxy News channel. She had read about the simulcast in the newspaper, but had rejected invitations from her new friends in the fast-growing Vancouver Resistance to join her for the screening.

She realized that this would be the last time she would ever see Winston, and she wanted to be alone with him. She lay back on the couch and braced herself.

Minister of Truth Russ Limetoff appeared at the podium and introduced, "An important message for God's United States from our President and courageous Commander-in-Chief, George O. Blush."

The small audience sprung to their feet and erupted with enthusiastic shouts of "GOB! GOB! GOB!"

President Blush took the podium wearing a dark blue suit with a red tie and white shirt, looking as though he had just returned from a good workout at the gym.

"Now you GOB-ers quiet down," he said, but the chants of "GOB! GOB! GOB!" rose instead. The President smiled like a good sport until his admirers grew still.

"Thank you, God bless you all, and God bless America!" The applause grew and died down again. "I am here this morning to tell you of another victory in our relentless war against terror and those who would do harm to our great country."

The President spoke for five more minutes, then turned the podium over to General Bashcrost. Bashcrost warned "those who would take advantage of our freedoms to promote their terrorist agendas" and reminded Americans of their legal duty to "report Subversives wherever and whoever they might be."

General Bashcrost told the nation that Homeland Security had uprooted a dangerous terrorist conspiracy that had managed to hijack, for three hours, America's emergency network so that they could simulcast hate speech against the government. Bashcrost said that Winston Smith, a pawn in this international conspiracy, "would like to use this opportunity to denounce his Islamic puppet-masters and apologize to the American people before he returns to the high-security solitary jail cell where he will remain for the rest of his life."

Winston was brought to the podium, looking lost and vacuous. A plastic surgeon had restored his face and hair to their original state, so viewers could recognize him as the same person who had been his government's most outspoken critic. A man whispered something in his ear. Winston looked straight ahead and started reading the speech from the teleprompter, without emotion and uncomfortably loudly.

Tears flooded Dawn's face as she ordered the TV to mute itself. She calmed herself down by rubbing a soothing ointment on the huge bulge beneath her ribs.

"That's not Winston, my little love," she whispered to the roundness in her middle. "That's not your father. I'll tell you about your father . . ."

The Revised Constitution of God's United States
A Patriotic Citizen's Bill of Rights and Responsibilities
(Passed by Congress and Ratified in 2009)

Preamble: We the people of God's United States, in order to provide for the common defense, in balance with the blessings of liberty and our position as the Freest Country on Earth™, do ordain the replacement of the Amendments of the Constitution of the United States of America, in accordance with law, and ratified as per the original, outdated Constitution of the United States, by two thirds of both Houses of Congress, as well as the Legislatures of three fourths of the fifty states, in the year of our Lord 2009, to hereafter be known as The Patriotic Citizen's Bill of Rights. The full force of the provisions of these Amendments are effective immediately, and the Judicial Branch of the Government of God's United States is hereby instructed to interpret any disparity between the original Articles of the Constitution and its original Amendments, and this revised and updated Patriotic Citizen's Constitution, in favor of the latter.

Amendment I: With the exception of the state-sanctioned religion of Christianity, Congress shall make no law respecting an establishment of any other religion or prohibit the private, non-subversive exercise of any religion. Nor shall Congress abridge the freedom of speech, or of the press; or the right of the people peaceably to assemble, and to petition the government for a redress of grievances; although the President and his appointed agents may do so, in Time of War, or serious threat of war or terrorism, to protect the Country and its people, as he, in his sole discretion, deems fit in the exercise of his duty as Commander in Chief.

Amendment II: A well-regulated militia, being necessary to the security of a free state of Patriotic Citizens, the right of the people to keep and bear arms, shall not be infringed, unless such people are suspected or actual abortionists, illicit drug users, subversives, terrorists, enemy sympathizers or propagandists, as determined by the Department of Homeland Security.

Amendment III: No soldier shall, in time of peace be quartered in any house, without the consent of the owner, nor in time of war, but in a manner to be prescribed by law, as determined by the President and Commander in Chief, and administered by the Department of Homeland Security.

Amendment IV: Except during Time of War, the right of the people to be secure in their persons, houses, papers, and effects, against unreasonable searches and seizures, shall not be violated, and no warrants shall issue, but upon probable cause, supported by oath or affirmation, and particularly describing the place to be searched, and the persons or things to be seized. During Time of War, as defined by the President and Commander in Chief, representatives of the Department of Homeland Security may take any and all measures necessary to search the homes, effects, electronic communications or records of suspected or actual abortionists, illicit drug users, subversives, terrorists, enemy sympathizers or propagandists, and it shall be a federal crime, as prescribed in federal criminal statute 841 (d) 1, as described in Patriot Act VI, to inquire about such searches, or to inform the subjects of such searches, or the public, of any actions taken under this statute by representatives of the Department of Homeland Security.

Amendment V: No person shall be held to answer for a capital, or otherwise infamous crime, unless on a presentment or indictment of a grand jury, except in cases arising in the land or naval forces, or in the militia, when in actual service in Time of War or public danger. With the exception of suspected or actual abortionists, illicit drug users, subversives, terrorists, enemy sympathizers or propagandists; no Patriotic Citizen shall be compelled in any criminal case to be a witness against himself, nor be deprived of life, liberty, or property, without due process of law; nor shall private property be taken for public use, without just compensation, unless deemed necessary by the President and Commander in Chief or the Department of Homeland Security.

Amendment VI: In all criminal prosecutions except those involving suspected or actual abortionists, illicit drug users, subversives, terrorists, enemy sympathizers or propagandists, Patriotic Citizens accused of crimes shall enjoy the right to a speedy and public trial, by an impartial jury of the state and district wherein the crime shall have been committed, which district shall have been previously ascertained by law, and to be informed of the nature and cause of the accusation; to be confronted with the witnesses against him; to have compulsory process for obtaining witnesses in his favor, and to have the assistance of counsel for his defense.

Amendment VII: In suits at common law which do not involve the Government of God's United States, Government officials, Party Members or Party Institutions, where the value in controversy shall exceed twenty dollars, the right of trial by jury shall be preserved, and no fact tried by a jury, shall be otherwise reexamined in any court of the United States, than according to the rules of the common law.

Amendment VIII: Excessive bail shall not be required of any Patriotic Citizen, nor excessive fines imposed, nor cruel and unusual punishments inflicted, with the exception of suspected or actual abortionists, illicit drug users, subversives, terrorists, enemy sympathizers or propagandists. Should abortionists, illicit drug users, subversives, terrorists, enemy sympathizers or propagandists be found guilty, by any state or federal court, of any criminal offense, then their voting privileges for any public election shall be permanently revoked.

Amendment IX: The enumeration in the Constitution, of certain rights, shall not be construed to deny or disparage such rights to unborn children, from the very moment God Almighty breathes life into their eternal souls. In any and all cases, including rape, incest, and health emergencies, any persons infringing upon the life of the unborn, whether mothers, relatives, health care providers, or their co-conspirators, shall be subject to the full force of state statutes concerning homicide or attempted homicide.

Amendment X: During Time of War the President, Vice President, and all other elected officials who are members of the Nationalist Party, the only Party found by the American people to be a Patriotic

Citizens Party, are exempted from federal, state and local term limit legislation, including Amendment XXII of the outdated Constitution of the United States, prescribing a two term limit to the Office of President.

In Time of War, as determined by the President and Commander in Chief, all political parties, with the exception of the Nationalist Party ("The Party"), are suspect and illegal until such Time of War has passed, and it shall be a criminal federal offense to lobby, propagandize, assemble, or vote for any political person or action that is not part of the official Party. It is henceforth the duty of all Patriotic Citizens to vote for and provide support to the Party, until such time as the President, in his sole discretion, determines that God's United States is no longer at war.

This Patriotic Citizens Constitution expands the rights, and responsibilities of Citizens in the following manner:

All Patriotic Citizens of the United States shall enjoy the right, and responsibility, of receiving and watching Interactive TV. Such responsibilities include an obligation to watch requisite public service announcements, as determined by the President in Time of War. It shall be a federal offense, in Time of War, to tamper with or disable the security delivery or monitoring functions of any Interactive TV device.

Patriotic Citizens are also entitled to an expanded right of Pharmacological Happiness, and all providers of health insurance must fully cover the cost of providing such Pharmacological Happiness. In the event that the Department of Homeland Security establishes, in it sole discretion, that a citizen is psychologically imbalanced, then representatives of the General of Homeland Security shall have the right, in Time of War, to define Pharmacological Happiness within the context of the needs of God's United States, and to medicate and/or genetically reform lawbreaking criminals as they deem necessary.